The Meteor Symphony: Stories and Poems

Debbie Burke

For those who dream in music

Table of Contents

Author's Note

Taking the Compilation Route

What started out as my fourth novel has become a compilation that includes eleven short stories, eighteen poems, and fourteen works of microfiction about music, life lessons, humor, and humanity, all reflecting my perpetual curiosity about the world we live in. Some of the material presented here is fiction, some is nonfiction.

The Meteor Symphony: Stories and Poems has been in the works for over a year. But there was a big epiphany in getting it into its current form. Let me give you some quick background.

The author experience has a tendency to leave me and many of my writerly colleagues hollow and tired. There is a "grind mentality" for creatives. We have several amazing online platforms to immediately get our words and ideas out to the world at the flick of a finger, not only on social media but also through the various online booksellers that are designed for authors to upload and publish on. It's a miracle! But it also creates pressure, much of which, for authors, is often self-induced.

The pace at which authors are advised to self-market while also writing Important and Engaging Books can be a coronary-in-waiting. I was stressing over making the title story "The Meteor Symphony" into a novel, but it seemed to hit its critical mass at short story length. None of my three full-length novels—*Glissando: A Story of Love, Lust and Jazz*; *Icarus Flies Home*; and *Death by Saxophone*—had any intentions of being released as short fiction, but there was something about "Meteor"...

I was enamored of the premise of the book/story, which centers on the early 1900s composer Gustav Holst's fictional undiscovered symphony and whose subplot originally included an "age-gap" romance. However, I felt that the relationship part of the story was becoming a distraction from the musical theme. Writing about limerence and falling in love is one of my favorite things, but I put those aside for the sake of keeping "Meteor" about one woman's exploration to find meaning in Holst's music.

I often have interesting ideas pop into my head when I'm on the cusp of falling asleep, and when I'm feeling determined, I'll rouse myself enough to stretch my arm over to the notebook on my nightstand and jot down a few words. I'm reminded of the *Seinfeld* episode where Jerry wakes up in the middle of the night to write down what he thinks is the punchline of a brilliant joke, only to be unable to read his own chicken scratch upon waking. This is why I write these nighttime snippets slowly and in a big, loopy handwriting (all in the dark, of course). These ideas, in turn, often get saved in a document I call "Prompts," to be revisited when the writing bug hits.

I hope you enjoy my latest exploration of jazz, poker, falling in love, sunsets, and life's amazing adventures.

Debbie Burke

2025

Short Stories

New York City Sax Heist

Sally Sue Cordella might be the most famous alto sax player you've never heard of. The fifty-two-year-old Brooklyn resident recently came into possession of a 1964 Aristocrat—a quite rare horn, etched curiously with not just the usual scrollwork on the ligature and body but also with images of circus animals and a calliope at the end of the bell. The dubious origin story of entering Sally Sue's possession, however, is a bit of a dark tale.

Steven Jay Price, whose radio show persona was just his last name, was wholly responsible for the afternoon-to-overnight programming on Brooklyn County Community College Radio Station WJZZ saw the tiniest snippet in the "About Town" section of the New York Post and nearly choked on his lemongrass kale shake. It read:

> *A Brooklyn-bound cabbie who picked up a "determined-looking" woman in Manhattan's Upper West Side was stunned when a passenger found an incredibly valuable saxophone in the back seat and refused to hand it over. "I never saw anything like this," he said, clearly shaken up. "She seemed nice enough, but when I suggested she hand it over to me so I could track down the owner, she told me no." His rude passenger then threw a ten-dollar*

bill over the front seat and got out at a red light, disappearing into the night. Police are investigating.

Price knew he had to find this woman and interview her on his show, if only to massage his soggy ratings. He put a plea out on the air. The daytime hosts also put the word out when they came into the studio.

As his luck would have it, all he needed to do was go on social media to see if anybody was bragging about having "found" the vagabond sax. A simple search ("lost sax NYC cab") got an immediate hit.

Sally Sue Cordello responded to Price's message on Instagram and agreed to come on the air, under one condition. No cops.

"Sure thing, Sally."

"Sally SUE."

At two in the afternoon the next day, Sally Sue set out for Brooklyn County Community College. Though technically only three miles away, she gave herself an hour (Brooklyn traffic being what it was) to find the entrance to the school and make her way to the right building.

As she approached the guard shack, she came to a stop, then rifled through her purse to get the security pass Price had emailed her. The guard nodded. "You'll go past the athletic field at your right. Communications is the next left from there. It's a small building with a statue of the school logo in iron. It's all rusted through. You can't miss it."

He doesn't know my sense of direction, she thought. *It's a stroke of luck that I got here in the first place.*

Sure enough, the building came into sight with its ruddy letters: "BCCC."

Price had called in a special favor from Neddy Johnson, the school's burliest security guard. Though Price didn't know if Sally Sue was or could be a threat, he knew one thing: anyone could make a weapon of an alto sax, in more ways than one. Better to be safe than sorry.

Sally Sue found the door with a peeling radio tower sticker on it and rapped three times. Price took a sharp intake of breath and nodded to Neddy, who was chilling with the latest copy of DownBeat. Then the radio host pulled the door open.

"Sally Sue?"

She felt satisfied he had gotten her name right.

"Yes, it's me."

Price smiled nervously and let her in. A black plastic trash bag apparently with the musical contraband swung into the steel door with a clunk, causing Sally Sue to giggle. Price tried not to look horrified.

When they settled into their seats, Sally Sue, who kept the bag on her lap, glared straight ahead. Not blinking, she asked, "So how does this work?" She turtled her head in to get a better look at the mic, phallic and covered in protective foam, just inches from her face. She fought the urge to push it away, out of her bubble of space. A slight sneer tugged at the right side of her mouth. *One more transgression, my dear Mr. Price,* she thought, *and I'm out of here.*

She softened when she realized Price was similarly crunched into his chair on the other side of a small steel desk with magazines and sticky notes of all hues. Calling the studio "modest" was an overstatement.

"Now remember, this is live, but with a seven-second delay. They used to call that a 'profanity delay,' so you get where I'm coming from." He looked at his guest. No reaction.

"First I'll introduce you to the listeners," he continued. "I'll frame it this way: you found a saxophone in a cab and today, you're here with it to tell us your story. Sounds good?"

Sally Sue shifted in her squeaky chair. "Um." She paused. "Okay. But you said no cops, not even campus security. So I'm free to tell it my way?"

Neddy was just outside in the hallway, eyes shielded by wraparound sunglasses. He peered into the sound booth. With his left hand, he drummed an imagined rhythm onto the carpeted walls, and with his right, he fingered the cell phone in the pocket of his black nylon vest. He gave a slow dip of his head, letting Price know he was watching everything unfold and he was at the ready to call in the troops if needed. Naturally, campus police had been told about Sally Sue's visit and were in the building, while two uniformed city cops sat outside in their car nearby, listening to WJZZ's canned music. "I Remember Clifford" played while Price queued up the show.

"You are totally free to tell it your way." Price smiled, happy that he was getting this scoop and determined not to blow it. It wasn't so much that he wanted an on-air confession, though that would do a lot to solidify his bona fides. What Price really wanted was a look at this saxophone. Its owner, an iconic sideman and soloist who was a three-time National Endowment of the Arts Jazz Master, made a plea on almost every social media platform for its safe return in exchange for a healthy reward. Price wasn't banking on the reward, but he did want to see the instrument. Maybe…she would let him try it out.

"And in five, four…" Price gestured the rest of the countdown with his fingers.

"Good afternoon, jazz lovers all over the beautiful borough of Brooklyn and beyond! Today, we have a very special guest." Price took a silent sip of water. "You might have heard about the sax that was 'misplaced' by a very famous musician and that somebody found in one of our yellow New York City cabs. Well, the recipient of that interesting fortune is here. Today, we're interviewing Miss Sally Sue Cordella. Thanks for coming in, Sally Sue!" He raised his eyebrows and lifted his chin for her to start.

"Good afternoon, Steven Jay!"

Price's left eye twitched. "So let's start right in with how you found this horn—"

"I think y'all know it's an *alto saxophone*." She drew the last two words out.

"Yes, well, generically, I sometimes refer to the sax as a horn. Or an axe. Or any number of things! But the one you found. Tell us, how did this get into your hands?"

"Thank you, and I must say this is a very small—dark, even—radio station. I've not been in a lot of them and had no idea they were this, uh, cave-like. Anyway, thank you for the privilege. And let me just say, this was a stroke of fortune! I never could have imagined this." Sally Sue sat back in her chair, lips sealed.

This was not going to be an easy interview. Price was just hoping there was somebody, anybody, listening. At 3 p.m., it was not yet drive time for commuters, and the station's stats had shown a consistently paltry market share for midafternoons. Most people seemed to tune in right after the traditional US/East Coast dinnertime hour with wine or weed (or both) in hand. He knew this because of the comments on the surveys. And the streaming listeners tuned in mostly at nighttime and then overnight. Three in the afternoon was a sonic wasteland. Jazz as an art form was not having its day in the sun.

"What street did you get the cab on and where were you going?" he asked, tone hopeful and encouraging.

"Oh, that! Those are the details you want. Okay!"

Neddy laughed into his hand and then gave his head a quick, hard shake. He pitied Price at this moment. He would definitely take the guy out for an IPA the next time they were both off. They were buds that way.

Price had only slotted in an hour for the interview, and the way things were going, it was looking like he wouldn't even fill that up. He had plenty of chestnuts to play, though, classic jazz songs that even casual fans enjoyed in case she turned out to be a dud.

"I got into the cab at 87th and Amsterdam. I was coming from a nice little vegan restaurant that I ended up eating alone at. I was supposed to have a date there but he ghosted me. Tinder, you've heard of it?"

Price blushed. Not because he knew the app well and had used it unsuccessfully for months (swearing just the other day how he'd be giving it up), but at the embarrassment over her candor. It was TMI.

"I have heard of it, yes. And so you hailed a cab?"

"Well, I ate first, anyway. Just because the schmuck was a no-show didn't mean I couldn't eat, did it?"

"Of course not."

Maybe this *would* take the full hour. Maybe even more.

"So I had my dinner, I don't think you need to know precisely what I ate, and then I started walking to the train station."

"And where do you live?"

"Well, I don't want to say."

"That's fair."

"Marine Park." She smiled ghoulishly.

Neddy turned his back on the booth and coughed. Price saw him slump down a little, laughing into his sleeve, then coming back up.

"So I almost got to the station. I saw the lights and was about to descend to the depths of subway hell, you know, haha!"

"Yes?"

"And I realized I felt safer in a cab. It was dark and cold and I just wanted to be delivered door to door. You know? Like, treat myself. Why not! I was just stood up. Self-care is everything."

"And the cab, well, who pulled over?"

"Oh, a very nice gentleman. It looked like he was from the Middle East. But I don't judge."

Red flag number three or four (he'd stopped counting) was flapping wildly in the wind at this point. That seven-second delay was about to come in handy, but he was dreading having to stop the show. The streams had tripled in the past five minutes and continued to tick upward.

"I know you don't judge, Sally Sue. You are a sensible and might I say a very interesting person!" His hand was poised over the red button of silence, just waiting for the next gem to drop. "Tell me about what you saw in the back seat," he prompted.

"I saw this beautiful serpentine sax, that you so crudely called a horn, on the back seat, sitting there, minding its own business. I gasped and must have said something out loud like 'Ooh, who left this here?' and before I could compose myself, the Irani, or maybe he was Arab or Jewish, I can't tell. I hope I don't offend anybody! But before I could stop myself, the cab driver who was headed south on Columbus Avenue—well, the light was still green and he actually turned around to look at me! I panicked, so I guess I kind of yelled at him to turn around and drive, for cripe's sake."

But did she steal it? mused Price.

"So I grabbed it by the neck, right? And waited for him to stop at the next red light. Then I threw a bill at him, I don't know if it was a ten or a twenty, because you know it's illegal not to pay your fare. I threw open my door and got out. We were in the middle lane, darn it, and I had to move fast before the light turned green. As it was, a bike rider nearly knocked me down."

"What did you do from there?"

"I hate to admit it, but I walked to the next subway station and went home."

"The sax? Was there a case?"

"No, it was just on the seat alone, naked, really, haha, so I hid it under my coat the best I could and jumped on the IND line. I live in a two-fare zone, as you know, so I have to take the Avenue R bus at the Kings Highway station to get back home. I'm not saying where I live, of course."

"What did you think you were going to do with the saxophone?"

Sally Sue let out a short, bark-like laugh. "I mean, what do you think? You think I know how to play this thing? Here, you play it." She shoved it at him.

This was his one and only chance. In a few minutes, he knew the sax and its temporary owner would be scurried along in their journey. Gingerly, Price took it from her and stood it up on his leg. The etching was beautiful, unlike anything he'd ever seen. He played clarinet a little bit, and he knew the sax had similar fingering.

"Can I play it?" Even as he said it, he understood how bizarre the situation was. But why not give it a toot before it was confiscated? Which, by his estimation, was going to happen pretty damn soon. Neddy had messaged him that things were about to happen and it came up as a little popup on Price's screen, which was turned away from Sally Sue's line of sight.

He used a wet wipe to rid the reed of any of the big germs (leaving the small germs very happily intact) and licked it to coat it with his own funky DNA, then began to blow. The thing played itself. The sound was full, round, warm, incredible. And it was criminal evidence. Remembering this, he quickly sampled a few bold arpeggios and then handed it back to Sally Sue.

"Whew! You sound great," she said. "Maybe you want this? I'll sell it to ya. Ha!"

The clock read forty minutes down, ten more to go. Hopefully, the cops would be there in that slim window. Rounding out the hour would be some Charlie Parker and then some Turrentine.

Coordinating this was Neddy's job. The man could be relied on 110%, so Price knew the end was definitely in sight.

Sally Sue had no idea what was going to happen, but then again, technically speaking, neither did Steven Jay Price.

"I have one more thing to say." She said it like it was a warning.

"Go ahead, we are all ears." It was true. At this point, sixty-three thousand pairs of ears. Unbelievable!

"It's just that, well, I know the owner misses his 'horn,' as you've called it."

This woman's elevator did not go to all the floors. That much was clear.

"And since I don't even play the thing, well, I'm prepared to let it go for a reward," she said. "Say, ten thousand smackeroos?"

"Oh, Sally Sue, that's not for me to decide," Price said flatly.

"Well, let's put it out for the highest bidder, then! Turn your radio show into an auction and let's get this happening! I don't have all day."

Sally Sue was looking agitated and frazzled. Price didn't know how long he could keep this up.

Just then, the light of day streamed into the studio and in strode two city cops. Price hit his red button and switched on his pre-recorded message. He'd prepared two of them.

The first pre-recorded spiel said something about "running out of time" and was to be used in case the interview went over the fifty minutes. Advertisers had paid for their spots and certain programming, and he would need to continue the interview offline, record it, and play it at a later time.

The second message was to be used in case something unexpected or violent happened, where he told the audience that due to technical issues, the interview had to be terminated, which was the option he used as the cops burst in and helped Sally Sue to her feet. Waiting in the wings was the owner of the saxophone, who happened to be in town promoting his retrospective album. He wept when he saw his instrument and threw Price a look of disgust that he'd dared to play it, immediately followed by a smile of understanding of what had transpired and that he himself would have done the exact same thing.

"So what do you think?" Benjy Grant, the relieved musician, asked Price. "Is she smooth or is she smooth?"

"Like an evening with a strong bourbon at a crackling fireplace."

"A poet. We should collab sometime."

Age-Gap Heart Attack

I flew into the ER waiting room wild-eyed. I recognized the receptionist. She was the one who signed my neighbor in when she was having chest pains.

"MARTIN?" I shrieked.

The receptionist looked at me, clearly tired but trying to be helpful. "Last name?"

"Powell." My heart was pulsing in my ears.

"Room 7. They just took him in for X-rays." She wasn't supposed to buzz me in without ID, but she did. I'd have to get this woman a tin of specialty cookies for this.

I ran through the double doors, coming in at Room 32, and followed the winding path to the lower numbers. Breathless, I caught up with Martin as he was being wheeled into his room. He was rubbing his face with his hands and groaning. He didn't see me.

The tech placed him by the bed, still in the wheelchair, then nodded to me and said, "Family?"

"His daughter."

Did I really say that?

His smile was perfunctory. I knew he didn't believe me. "Have a seat. Mr. Powell will be waiting for the doctor." Then he left.

"Hannah! How did you find me?"

"My supervisor told me, HIPAA be damned."

"It certainly is. Or at least, it should be."

I took his hand and brought it to my lips, thus far the most intimate gesture between us. But we both knew there were sparks before this. He smiled weakly.

"Hannah... Really. What do you want with an old man like me?"

I gently let go of his hand and eased onto the edge of the bed. It was a small room, this number 7.

"Whatever you'll give me."

For once, the loquacious scholar was silent. I'd stunned him.

"Look," he said. "I already have a daughter, so you can't be that. I already have an ex-wife, and you definitely don't want to be that." He let out a sharp laugh.

"I'm sure that's a story and a half."

"I won't bore you with my history."

"What do you want to bore me with?" I asked.

"You're adorable. How about a cup with ice chips?"

"Sure thing. Back in a jiffy."

Martin Cedric Powell was a quietly confident man who happened to have circled the sun forty-one more times than me. What was I getting myself into?

I knew that whatever role I was about to play better be something I was committed to because getting involved and then later changing my mind, even though I was certainly allowed to do whatever I wanted, would not aid in his recovery.

I had to figure this out fast...if love was crackling around the edges of us or if this was just me, selfishly flirting with the idea of flirting.

Finding ice chips was the easy part.

Middle School Love

That summer, I found out that I was a lovable person. What a gift.

He was a fellow eighth-grader I didn't even give a second glance to. One day, he followed me home from orchestra practice. In those days, no cell phone, no pepper spray, just pure obliviousness. Innocence. But also, freedom from worry.

I was working out Handel's "Water Music" (second movement) in my head. We were going to perform it on the boardwalk at the Coney Island Aquarium. He was not an orchestra kid but a debating team kid, so I guess he loved himself a little slice of classical music. From the skinny little girl with pigtails, the hair ties with clear plastic balls on them. Just a-swingin' my violin case on the B44 bus to get back home, stuffing my bus pass holder deep in my stretch pants so it wouldn't be stolen. Nostrand Avenue could be a rough place.

I hadn't realized he was on the same bus since it was packed. But when I got off the bus using the back stairs, I sensed somebody behind me.

He got off at my stop but stayed back about half a block. I knew at that point he was following me home, but I wasn't alarmed because I turned and waved and he smiled back.

I walked down along the new buildings of Brooklyn College, and he saw me turn onto East 23rd Street. Almost home, then down the block to Glenwood Road.

Ultimately, he asked me out. Our first date was at the movie called *The Seven-Ups* with Roy Scheider. We spent a lot of time walking around the college campus, watching them build new handball courts. At first, he used my nickname all the time, teasingly and warmly. Then, gradually, he stopped calling me anything.

When, three months later, he ghosted me—that would be what we'd call it forty years later—he did double damage, breaking my heart and leaving me in a world of confusion.

When I was not sixteen anymore, the heartbreak served up a valuable lesson. There's a moment when you know whether you can trust another person with your love.

Listen carefully.

Watching for the Sunset

It was time to put the house up for sale. Suzanne had prepared for months for this moment, ever since Jack got his diagnosis. From the moment the doctor had called them to deliver the bad news, Jack's decline was swift. He was gone in two weeks. Barely enough time for her to process what was happening.

She decided she wouldn't continue to live in this house; it held too many memories and every step would be a heartbreaking reminder of his absence.

The tidy 1,300-square-foot home would undoubtedly sell fast in the growing little ocean-adjacent town of Pillory, Virginia. She priced it under market. The inheritance from her father's estate never had to be touched because Jack's businesses had done so well over the years. A candy empire, that was what Jack dreamed of building, and he did just that.

With Jack gone in early October, Suzanne made some calls and connected with a friend of a friend, a knowledgeable and respected local realtor named Janet Hize. The house was listed in November, and before the fresh scent of spring hit the air, there was an offer. There would be help for her next phase. She had two grown sons who coordinated their schedules to help her pack up her things. "This will be my last home sweet home," she said with a sad smile.

It was an age-in-place community that started out as a co-op. Services and care could be added as needed, sometimes with a physical move to the main building for those who met an unfortunate deterioration. But Suzanne didn't want to think about that. She was perfectly capable of driving her little Swedish car, choosing her own groceries, loading the trunk with bags, and putting them away in her pantry and kitchen. And she would continue to do this in her new home. She was a self-reliant woman thus far unencumbered by physical ailments.

The small co-op was set in a walled-off neighborhood complete with supermarket, glass-bricked coffee shop, and hardware store, plus a cheap cab service built in, making it possible to one day ditch her car. When that time came, her older son Tomas would take care of selling it. He was always the more practical one, organized and methodical, efficiently navigating his way through life. His brother

Jonathan was drawn to the more physical tasks: boxing up his mother's belongings, then carrying her big brown furniture around the new apartment, placing dressers and cabinets here and there until Suzanne was satisfied that everything was in the right place. Tomas and Jon worked till their shirts were heavy with sweat, putting everything where she wanted it, and they called for takeout.

Up until Jack got sick, their social life was always aflutter, thanks to his natural gregariousness that was his company's secret sauce. He always joked that it was his gift of gab that built his business, not the delicious chocolate that he imported from all corners of the globe. When freight and politics made international business impossible ("impassable," he'd called it), he looked around at a life built by sweets and decided enough was enough. At exactly sixty-five years old and a day, he sold the business to a cracker company that assimilated it into its larger-scale corporation.

She missed Jack like a limb lost in a war and because of it was never able to sleep in their bed again. She invested in a high-end recliner and woke up every morning determined to stay cheerful. It was an act, but for whom?

There was an agenda for each day. She had purchased ten sturdy spiral-bound 6 x 9 journals where she penned in her daily instructions, no more than three for any given day, so she could always hit her mark. Whether it was bookkeeping chores that had to be done or small household tasks, each item was always checked off by dinnertime. Ever since high school, this method had worked for her. When times were bad, it was the one thing she could count on. The notebook was not a diary but living proof that she made a small ripple in the ocean of humanity. She had some impact, no matter how brief or tiny.

In the morning, she faced a fresh page with confusion. It was her first full day here. There was so much to do, but also, absolutely nothing to do, what with Jack not around and no friends.

Her new kitchen held traces of the scent of fried rice from dinner the night before with her boys. The last time they were all together was at Easter. She wished they could be together more often. *I'll take what I can get,* she thought. *Plenty of other widows have nobody. I have no reason to complain.* And even though she'd just lost Jack, she considered herself immensely blessed. An amazing sixty-seven years with the love of her life.

Her phone chimed. It wasn't a familiar ringtone. The name displayed as HIZE. The realtor?

"Suzanne," the cigarette-roughened voice said flatly. "It's Janet Hize."

This was a surprise.

"Janet? How are you? Is everything okay?"

A cough, then, "Yes, very much so. The new owners are in love with your home. You took such good care of it and they're going to be very happy."

"That's good to know. I was so worried about selling the house and moving, but you did a great job. It was painless!"

"That's what I'm here for." Another cough. "There's something I wanted to talk to you about."

This sounded ominous. Suzanne sat on her familiar couch, now overlooking the oak tree-lined streets where the other widows and widowers lived. What could be wrong? Her temples pulsed.

"The new owners found some letters and were just wondering if you wanted them back. They were actually in a side panel in the second bedroom closet."

Letters? Suzanne didn't know about any letters. She'd taken all the cards and other correspondence from Jack to her new home. By force of habit—or sentimentality—she looked through them every day since Jack was gone. The ritual hadn't changed in her new apartment.

"Oh, those," Suzanne said, as if knowing about them all along. "You can trash them."

"You're sure you don't want them?"

"It's fine. Thanks for asking. Now, if I left any jewelry, by all means, forward it on."

"Okay then," Janet said slowly.

"Thanks again, and have yourself a good day!" Suzanne said brightly.

A still-steaming mug of fresh coffee lent its aroma to the sunny dinette.

"Jack," she said out loud, a hint of a smile on her lips. "I hope you're having fun frolicking up there. Just remember, one day, we'll be together again."

She looked around at the photos that her sons had thoughtfully arranged on the ledge over the TV. Good times, good years. Nothing could erase that.

"But don't wait up, Jack," she continued. "I'm in no hurry, and I have some adventure left in me. I'll be fine."

She found her newest notebook and started writing. She added one extra item for the day and underlined it:

4. Find out if they have a beauty parlor here

Missing the Vine

The nursing home has the smells and personality that you would expect. There's a nice dollop of surliness, enough so you know you're not in a luxury hotel, and thank God for that (I could never afford it). However, truthfully, for all these staff people put up with, there is mostly cheer and patience and friendly banter. I have no reason to start getting nasty and negative with people now when I've been pretty happy-go-lucky all my life. In turn, I'm shown respect and care.

When they roll me into the cafeteria, I ask them to position me at a window seat. There are no assigned tables, but they know my favorite couple of spots. I look out onto Sheepshead Bay and watch the worn-out fishing boats spill their silvery wares onto the splintered wooden piers. They sell out every day by noon. Lots of Italians and Portuguese in this neighborhood and they love their fresh fish. I haven't had fish in ages, unless you talk about shrimp, fried nicely, dipped in creamy tartar. Nothing else like it.

Besides the bay slapping the sides of the pier, I also hear the constant traffic and aggressive attitudes with the occasional fight over a parking space and watch the nannies pushing strollers, the bicyclists and skateboarders, the lovers and dog walkers.

If I'm lucky enough to get a visitor (and that would be my son or my daughter), they bring me some goodies from any one of the neighborhood delis. I like the fat rainbow-sprinkled cookies dipped in chocolate, but I will accept an éclair or a brownie. I also like a nice hot Lipton tea, no cream or sugar, in a double cup (because it's scalding) decorated with Greek geometric patterns. Then I really feel like a New Yorker.

I made a few friends, if you can call them that: people you nod to or share a ride in the elevator with. There have been times a nice-looking gentleman walked carefully with his cane, nodded his head at me when I was bay-gazing, and started a conversation. I'm not averse to that. I mean, it's nice to have somebody to give a smile to. But don't bother trying to flirt with me. Just conversation, thank you.

I was loved well and often, and I miss my husband. He's been gone fifty years now. What we did most was laugh. That was the secret to a long and happy marriage. There are other necessary ingredients, but trust me, humor is numero uno, without a doubt. He didn't slip off gradually. It was a terrible ordeal. To watch somebody battle an aggressive illness is not what any of us deserves, least of all this man, who was good and faithful and a wonderful friend and partner.

He'd been more adventurous than me. I never wanted to go skydiving or parasailing or ziplining. I'd be petrified of forgetting to grab onto a vine and that would send me plummeting below. Even the word "plummet" scares the crap out of me.

My kids don't live nearby so I appreciate the time and inconvenience they willingly take on to visit. They love the New York cookies just as much as I do. And guess what— we laugh all the time.

No grandkids, but that's their choice, and if I've learned anything it's to avoid being a pain in someone's tushy and leave them the hell alone with their personal lives. I certainly don't like people poking into mine.

Today I see there's going to be tomato soup and grilled cheese. Everything on the menu is pretty bland but I'm allowed to salt my food (I'm one of the few here without hypertension, and despite privacy guidelines, everybody, and I mean EVERYBODY, talks about not just their own illnesses but everyone else's). The only thing wrong with me, and the reason I'm here, is that my body has stubbornly decided to stop cooperating. I can't get around too well and they tell me that the damage from the thyroid cancer has compromised my general health. So it's a slow fade. Though the man I love didn't get that luxury (God knows that I would have traded places with my sweetie in a second, but my request was denied), he took his ending as well as you can expect. We were all there, my kids and his sisters and myself, seated or standing around him on his favorite couch at home with hospice care when the lights went out. He squeezed my hand and smiled and that was that.

You have to expect to lose people if you live a long life. That's just how it goes. Did you make great memories? For damn sure I did. I had some rocky years where I didn't handle myself the best, but I learned from my mistakes and righted wrongs and made amends.

There are sirens all the time here, night and day. It's part of the acoustic landscape of Brooklyn and so be it. I'll be here until I'm not, looking for the right vines to swing on.

Seasons

The Wing-Ding Diner was Featherton's last bastion of great *bad* American food. It was no wonder I was soothing my bruised post-breakup soul with a big heaping plate of well-done fries with gravy and a bacon cheeseburger—the Cardiac Arrest Special.

I'd been broken up with before. But this time felt like a turn of the page. I wasn't going to grovel and twist myself into a pretzel to make things fit. I'd seen this coming yet refused to get out of the way of the freight train heading straight for me.

Warren Drago, now my ex, had found somebody new. My spidey senses told me this was going on for a while, but with work so nuts and my dad in hospice, I couldn't mentally take on another thing. Though Warren's timing couldn't be worse—I was sure Dad's days were seriously numbered—I was actually relieved when my boyfriend passed by the bathroom as I was filling in my eyebrows and said those dreaded words.

"I'm giving back your key."

As I pressed a little harder with the makeup brush, making my right eyebrow too dark, I nodded quietly and stood, about to cry. As I said…from relief.

Warren and I loved each other but belonged in different worlds. Mine was a faithful partner world and his was not.

I dipped my seventh or eighth gravy-laden steak fry into a bit of ketchup and swirled it around. Warren had in fact left the key in the mail dish and waltzed right out of my life. It apparently had given me a huge appetite.

As I contemplated next steps, which were not to attend to my broken heart but rather getting my father's financial affairs in order, a man two booths away caught my eye. He didn't smile so much as allow the straight line of his lips to relax upward a degree. He looked from my left eye to my right, breathed in, and went back to his phone. He, too, was eating fries.

I considered all the things on my spreadsheet that had yet to be done. I still had a few questions about Dad's possessions. My plan was to finish filling my belly and then drive to the facility twelve miles away. I had my laptop so I could work if he fell asleep.

I loved being a call center operator in the insurance claims department. It gave me the flexibility to work anywhere at any time. The pace sometimes got intense, one phone call immediately following the other, but I remembered I could put my feet up and do the job in bed or on my couch and have a snack nearby. The company paid me overtime whenever I volunteered for it, so I could regulate my finances based on how much I wanted to work. And sometimes the hours leaked into the evenings, which was great for a person with insomnia.

I was now on my own for rent, but I'd only need a few extra gigs a month to make it work. I hated to think this way, but the upcoming inheritance from Dad would certainly help. Maybe I could finally buy my own place and be done with the iffyness of being a renter.

My father's face flushed with joy as I stood in his doorway. He stretched his neck toward me so I could kiss his cheek. I patted his hand on the bed. It was icy and riddled with age spots. I remembered strong hands pushing me on the swings and hands that gently rubbed my shoulders when I was sick with a fever. Hands that carried his big green accounting ledgers to the kitchen table where he tallied his numbers to see how much he'd made each week in the old hardware store he took over from his father.

"Are you staying for a while?" he asked in a thin voice. His smile was weak but hopeful and his lidded eyes a pale, watery blue.

"I sure am."

"Ya hungry?"

I told him about the fries. I told him somebody flirted with me.

"And what about your boyfriend? Didn't you tell me you might be, uh, getting married soon?"

I did not, but I wasn't going to pour cold water on his optimism.

"I have a tux somewhere at home," he added. "You can roll me down the aisle in that contraption over there—" he gestured to his wheelchair—"so I can give you away properly. You have to let me give you away."

A sigh and a single nod from me conveyed everything. We always had this unspoken understanding.

"You split up?"

"Yes, Dad. He was…. Well, he met somebody else."

My father straightened up and tried to raise his fist but couldn't get his elbow off the bed. "You tell that WARREN—"

"Dad." I gently guided him back into his pillow. "Look at me. I'm not upset. He wasn't the one."

"Oh."

I saw a tear slide down his cheek. I wiped it away for him like he'd done for me so many times. My father was the emotional one, not my mom. She was wrapped a little tight, but her love language was different. She helped me develop into a focused and efficient person who had the confidence to tackle any challenge. I was incredibly lucky that each parent gave me valuable gifts that made me into the successful and happy person I was today.

One person always loves more than the other does, and in my parents' case, it was my dad loving my mother more. He burned with it, helpless in her flames. He adored her. He cajoled her when she seemed down or too serious, he went to lengths throughout their marriage to entertain her and buoy her spirits.

I stayed with my father for several hours. He slept on and off. The hospice staff came and checked in with him. He seemed comfortable with them and peaceful about his current situation. So all in all, it was okay.

I didn't know how long his state of in-betweenness would go on, but I was grateful for this place. The long-term care policy he insisted on purchasing for himself when my forty-nine-year-old mother passed from a heart attack made sense. It was one of the last good policies, and it did a lot to cover his care here. Just about the only thing my dad complained about were the meals; they tasted like "cardboard boxes laced with Elmer's glue," he said. That was just a function of his gradual loss of appetite, but there was no need to go into explanations. Dad knew he was dying, and I wanted to give him all the grace I possibly could.

He was asleep, maybe for the night, so I blew him a kiss, said goodbye to the second-shift nurse, and left. I hurried to my car in the sprawling parking lot. November was the pathway to the guillotine of December. Once the current year was chopped off, the New Year might hold some hope. I didn't think Dad would make it, but he'd had a good run.

I dialed up the seat warmers and turned on the heating vents full force. I put on the Sinatra channel and sang along to "I've Got You Under My Skin." I love the crescendo when the band goes wild.

My mind wandered and I recalled the day and how much had happened in the span of less than twelve hours. My feelings for Warren had started to fade out months ago, but I was too cowardly to face it. It was more of an ennui than a true connection. I was in love with him once, but too much time had passed without passion, without fire. I was okay letting him go.

When I got home, I noticed the note he'd left earlier near the mail dish that held his apartment key.

I'll be back once more to finish getting my things, but I'll call you first to make sure it's okay. Prolly by the weekend. I really do still love you and I'm sorry for how things worked out.

No you're not.

One day, maybe soon, I thought, I would allow a moment of flirtation at a luncheonette to develop into something more. Warren had not chosen his exit at the best of times, but I didn't want any part of a hollow relationship;

we'd clung to the idea of us long enough. Next time, I'm going for the fire, I thought.

Sisters: A Dance for Two

Camille had a rough childhood and felt unfairly burdened by her younger sister Meredith's mental illness. Why was it always her responsibility to solve her sister's issues? That was what brought her to therapy.

Not that Camille had never availed herself of the opportunity before. She had sought help for a litany of things: her father's violent alcoholism and abandonment; her mother's quick rise in her career to provide for her two children while, after hours, being cloyingly co-dependent on Camille; and of course Camille's predictably horrible choice in men, over and over. This included an affair she entrenched herself in so deeply that it took years to see the constant microaggressions in that equation, and by then, it was too late. The guy died, taking with him all chances of Camille straightening out their torridly toxic dance for two.

No, her reentry into therapy was because the situation was becoming intolerable. Now age fifty to Meredith's forty-four, Camille could do no more to make life bearable for her sister. "You're on your own!" she screamed one Christmas, informing Meredith to take a cab from the hedge-ensconced upper-crust town in New Jersey where

Camille and her kids lived back to Meredith's hovel of a walk-up on 11th Avenue in New York City. The holidays always seemed to bring out the worst in families, Camille thought; each year, something mind-blowingly stressful would emerge and have her questioning her motivation for continuing the charade of blissful family togetherness.

Camille found a brand-new therapist as her old practitioner had retired. She was covered for up to twelve sessions per calendar year. Were there a need for more therapy in that time frame, one would have to explain new circumstances that brought the patient to seek additional support. Juliet Kascow, LCSW, encouraged Camille to give things with her sister "one more try" so she could know she did everything possible to mend their ancient rift. "You've gone no-contact for several weeks," the therapist mused aloud. "It feels to me like you might be strong enough to go back into the lion's den and see if the lion has made some progress."

"If I get eaten alive, I'm coming back for reparations." Camille was only half joking. She'd definitely fire her therapist if things didn't work out.

Meredith had taken New Jersey Transit to visit her sister for the weekend. It was a risk to invite her over again, Camille realized, but at least they had some fun things planned (a Korean scrub spa, the local dog park, a sip 'n' paint) to distract them from the barbed wire-bound emotional landscape they operated in.

Meredith had suffered through a series of unsuccessful remote customer service jobs covering everything from dental equipment to construction supplies to food safety and was about to job-hop (i.e., get fired) once more. There was one glimmer of light. She'd dabbled her whole life in the arts and was actually pretty good at it. Her photos of abandoned urban settings, or "URBEX," as it was called, even sold occasionally on online arts and home décor platforms. And then Camille made a misstep.

"Why not try flea markets? You can get a lot of exposure that way. It's not just old lamps and military buffs, you know. You might sell some more photos."

Meredith's nostrils widened. "I'm not just going to fling my photos out to the masses like grapes to crows," she announced cryptically. "If they come to my table and are seriously interested in them as art, not just to match a loveseat, that's a different story. I need to know my art is appreciated and I charge what they're worth. I never give them away for free. I don't know why my own sister would even suggest that."

"I wasn't suggesting that!" Camille bit her cheek, realizing she had once again risen to the bait. She was tired, existentially; she wouldn't be able to keep her emotions in check. Not anymore. It had been an awful time in her life. Her husband, an emotional vampire, finally moved out to be with his sidepiece (she never saw it coming), and right before that, she lost her best friend to politics. They just couldn't bear to be around each other. "To hell with 2016," she mumbled. "And every year since then."

Meredith perked up. "What?"

"I was referring to my life. How things changed so quickly a few years ago. I'm still adjusting." It annoyed Camille to have to explain this; her own sister should have remembered what a terrible time it was. "You might remember Tommy walking out on me? And at the same time, Golda dropping me for how I voted?"

"You were dropped because you're droppable."

"Oh, that's so perfect. Merry, I mean this in the best way and in the worst way. You can get the hell out of my life right about now."

She meant it but it terrified her at the same time. Meredith was always dancing around the lacy threat of hurting herself, but that was a control tactic. Camille had no fight left in her. Meredith would do as she wished, whether that included hastening her own demise or doing something else self-destructive — arranging dangerous hookups on social media, running her bank account into the ground with online auctions gone amok, or taking in stray cats… *Take your pick*, Camille thought.

Meredith was a forty-four-year-old mess who would never seek the help she so desperately needed, and no matter what Camille might do, Meredith could never be coaxed (or threatened for that matter) into getting the help that was, truly, a matter of life and death.

A completely different tactic suddenly popped into Camille's head. She almost said it as if in a dream state. The emotional fatigue had left a little door open that said "try this."

"Remember when you'd hear Mrs. DeSanto playing piano through the wall and you'd immediately stop whatever you were doing to listen? And that would make you want to grab a pencil and start sketching?"

"You always bring that up."

"I never bring that up," she said sadly. "But I am now. Point being, you were able to distract yourself from your pain. Doesn't photography do that for you now?"

Meredith's face fell. She was tired too. Down to her bones. "Yes, it does. But I really hate digital photography; it seems contrived. And I just can't afford the film and the chemicals anymore. I dismantled the darkroom in my apartment years ago."

"It was a great outlet for you."

"It was."

Which was probably the first time they'd agreed on anything in a long, long time.

"What if we figured out what Mrs. DeSanto played?" Camille proposed. "The song. It felt religious, maybe."

"How would you know!" Spittle formed at the corners of Meredith's mouth.

Just calm her down, thought Camille. "Let's try an experiment," she said evenly.

"I'm listening." Somehow, it was a warning. Meredith flopped onto Camille's bed and gathered all the pillows around her, building a low fortress. Camille was smart enough to allow it without comment. Then, eyes downcast, she slowly slipped over to her puffy club chair, giving Meredith plenty of space.

"I think I can hum it pretty well," Camille offered, picking up her phone. "Let's see if AI can tell us what it is."

"You're the expert."

A series of vertical lines like erect grass showed up on Camille's screen as she hummed the tune. *Keep going*, the app encouraged.

Camille only knew a few bars and repeated them two more times. Would it be enough?

"Ah, it's *Abide with Me* by the Scottish composer Henry Lyte in 1847. Do you—"

"Click on it. I want to hear it."

The link to YouTube yielded a chorus of soaring female voices that brought goosebumps to both women. For just a moment, they shared something that wasn't about their relationship.

"Well, DeSanto was a crazy lady anyway," Meredith said. "She yelled at us when we went trick-or-treating and threatened that she'd call the cops if I didn't stop ringing her doorbell. On Halloween!"

"But I mean, you liked hearing her play through the wall. Maybe there's something there," Camille suggested.

Meredith scratched her arms abruptly and shook her head from side to side. A throwback to her old tics.

And we're off. Camille stiffened up.

"So you're telling me that, *one*, I need to be 'fixed,' and *two*, now you're an expert in music therapy." Another few arm scratches from Meredith.

Camille had given it a shot. There was no use keeping this going. Besides, she was worn out. When did she get to have her way? It was always about Meredith.

The conversation had nowhere else to go and Camille remembered the "lion's den" comment she'd made to her therapist. "I'm exhausted. I'm taking myself to bed," she said.

For once, Meredith didn't have a snappy rejoinder.

"We'll pick up on this tomorrow, then," Meredith managed.

No doubt, thought Camille. *I'm sure we will.*

A Mossy Flavor

He slipped into the coffee shop like a prowler leaves the shadows, a grim look on his roadmap-lined face. Preoccupied, probably.

Something about him struck me like the pluck of a high string on a ukulele. I happened to look up at him the moment he spun around after paying for his black-no-sugar coffee and something approaching a smile flashed on his face. Then he was gone into the bluster of a new autumn.

I finished my hot chocolate at the long farm table. I preferred a two-top, but they were all taken.

The ritual of spending several hours at this tiny coffee hub every day was comforting. Besides a calico named Jorge, I had nobody to come home to. The staff here was made up of sweet, optimistic Millennials. They didn't care how long somebody like me hung out and used it as an office. As a good patron, I always came with a few extra singles to stuff into their tip jar. I was helping define the vibe of the place as a welcoming haven for the thirsty, the retired, the work-from-homers.

A week later, on a Thursday, Mr. Blustery Fall came in again. I straightened up and shot him a very unsubtle glance with my own hint of a smile. This time, his eyes sparkled.

I liked his overcoat. So New England, so professorish. It was a college town, so maybe he was one. Or maybe a playwright. But he could have been a seafood manager or a funeral director; it didn't matter. I'd look at him the same way because there was just something about him.

Before he left, he stopped to sip his coffee. Then he looked at me over his wire-rimmed glasses and nodded. I couldn't tell if that signaled that he approved of the coffee or of me.

Then he walked out.

I wondered whether this was just his day to buy coffee out. I would come back here next Thursday to see; Jorge wouldn't mind. But who was I kidding. I was here every day.

There was a lot I needed to do at home. Straightening out my artistic life was one of them. With all the time and equipment I'd invested in my cyanography, a niche area of photography using a special coated paper and copious amounts of sunlight, I'd done nothing to try to establish my name in this little hamlet since I moved here almost a year ago.

Unfortunately, the arts council that had helped give me a huge step up in exposure had, in one fell swoop, suddenly turned against me after a new executive director took the helm. She found my latest series of images too controversial and voted me out of several exhibits. It was pretty clear this was about politics. Either you were a favored son or daughter or you weren't; Ruthie Sodin wasn't having my open commentary about the arts' general incestuousness, thus actually proving my point. So in her pathological and insecure little way, she turned the group against me.

To be honest, my art was beautiful. Compelling, even. Since starting down this particular path, something I first learned about on Life and the Arts cable channel in 2009, I received kudos very early on. I got nice ink in the local and regional papers where I was living at the time, a few TV interviews, and things started to sell. Big time. A 16 x 20 photo of pine cones and skyscrapers was my biggest windfall to date, a commission that paid more than four months' rent, and when word got out to the buyer's network, it was abruptly followed by interest from National

Geographic. They'd paid handsomely for the image, and I was actually invited to be the cover artist for their April 2014 issue. Sales then shot through the roof, made possible not so much by my talent (present, yes, but not the main reason for my sales); my "instant success" was due to having snagged an excellent agent who knew precisely how and where to market me. Chevy-Ann Glitters (thank her hippie parents) nearly made me a household name.

Once the other artists let that despicable Sodin turn them against me, the arts council stopped choosing my art for their exhibits and contests. I tumbled, not prettily, from my pedestal. By then, Chevy-Ann Glitters was suffering long-term COVID and had taken a hiatus from the biz. Whatever I'd learned from her was a mere dot on the butt of a housefly compared to her insider's knowledge and connections. So that plus the local scene's sudden distaste for me brought me to a state of deflation, and I no longer wanted to create.

Practically overnight, cyanography became my not-mainstay. I got back into the medical field, where I sat, small and quiet, ignoring the potential joy held captive in the jugs of photo developer that lived in my closet. Today, although

I had Jorge, who was really too affectionate to be a cat, I craved human validation. Working from home as a medical transcriptionist certainly did nothing to get me out and about to meet new people. Jorge—intuitive and needy, like me—sensed my depressed state and spent more of his time trotting over and sitting in my lap. Soon enough, I realized I was perseverating on it, on the art community's collective meanness.

Sometimes, when you hit a creative block, it's time to take a break. I felt great when I was shooting, but my pictures lacked inspiration. My break came in the form of taking on extra hours at work, which of course meant at home. Nevertheless, it was time to get the local arts scene out of my brain.

Over the weekend, I made myself a little plan. I had about $3K more to go to pay off my car, not quite a piece of crap but getting there. It wasn't my fault; I'd bought it used. But I pampered it like crazy so it wouldn't become a full-fledged piece of crap. With the extra time working, I could pay it off sooner, and then have the means to get back into my photography or go in a completely different direction.

Sundays were usually clean the house and hang out on the couch with Jorge day, but something drew me to the coffee shop again. As usual, Jorge wasn't pleased to see me reach for the door, but I apologized, scratched his little orange and white head, and told him I wouldn't be long.

I took my laptop with me, but this time, it wasn't to log in and work. Personal research, that was my goal. I needed to shake up my routine and think about what I'd really like to do next. It could be another kind of artistic endeavor or maybe something completely different.

I was back for my habitual hot chocolate and ordered a larger size with whipped cream. When I unzipped my wallet to pay, I heard the person behind me in line say, "Fancy meeting you here."

Mr. Blustery Autumn—apparently, he also drank coffee on non-Thursdays—was smiling, looking dapper in his academic threads. He required no more from me than a smile in return, which I gave without weighing its potential outcome. Then, musky and aromatic cocoa in hand, I ambled to the back of the store and opened my laptop.

I'll admit, it was kind of a thrill to see him again. He was as attractive as I remembered, and I had in fact given him some thought over the past few days. A lot of it. But I didn't want to scrap my purpose for being there and I didn't want to be rude, so I just let the chocolate goodness warm me up as I stared at my desktop. I hadn't even logged onto the internet yet when I saw him stop at the table in front of me.

Just a nod, and then, as he shrugged off his houndstooth coat, he said two words in a gravelly voice: "Happy surfing."

I was glad he sat with his back to me. It took the pressure off. This way, there was no expectation of a conversation and I was free to roam about the internet.

I was distracted by a few stray molecules of scent that wafted over to me. There was something very earthy about it: warm, familiar, grassy. Well, I was done. There was no self-exploration to be had and no chance I could focus on what I came here for. I snapped the laptop shut. Maybe too noisily.

The professor turned around and smiled. "I hope I've not been a distraction. I'm only staying to finish my cuppa." He held up his coffee and tipped it my way. "Are you writing a book, if you don't mind my asking?"

"Not a writer. I'm trying to figure out my next steps in life."

His face went slack. "Sorry to have bothered you. You seem to have some very important things on your mind." Then he turned back around.

Life is short. Either I wanted to explore this obvious curiosity I felt about him or I needed to get down to business and figure my stuff out.

"You smell like moss, but in a good way," I called to him. "Are you a farmer?"

He nearly choked on his coffee as he turned back to me. "Not at all," he said, a toothy smile revealing years of excellent dentistry. "Must be my cologne. I'm an electrical engineer. I work in power generation. Windmills."

I scooped up my puffy nylon jacket and laptop, walked over to him, and pulled out the chair facing him. "Do you mind if I sit here?"

He was as surprised as I was at this.

"Please." He gestured to the chair.

"I'm Annie," I said. "I was...wait, I am. A cyanographer."

It sounded pretentious, but it was true.

"A who?"

"It's a kind of photography."

"Oh, I think I've heard of it. Like Man Ray."

"Kinda-sorta. Yes."

The minutes flew by as he talked about windmills and solar flares and I talked about sunshine on photographic paper.

There was a lull in the conversation as I noisily sipped up the last of my hot chocolate. I considered buying a replacement; I also thought about dipping out of there. There's nothing as awkward as a welcome that's been overstayed.

I gathered my jacket, my hands making my decision before my brain did. "It was great to meet you."

"You too, Annie. Take good pictures."

I took a step in the direction of the exit and then reversed. "And here I thought Thursday was your day," I said impulsively. "Well, next time you stop in, feel free to save me a seat. But no promises."

The scent of the forest was gone. In its place, I hoped, I'd left a few of my own molecules. Cocoa, with a dash of intrigue.

Thou Shalt Not

The buzz was that our accountant, Robert Wheatfield, had written a manifesto and emailed it throughout the department. I was not the least surprised since I'd had a run-in with him on my first day, when he came inappropriately close to—he claimed—"read my badge" and then demanded to know my last name. Petrified, I reported this to my supervisor, who might as well have waved it off with a laugh. "Typical Robert Wheatfield," she said. *Oh, so this is what I should expect?* I wondered, still shaken.

I worked in the art department of a PR firm. My friend and fellow graphic designer Bernadette made fun of him every time he came through our office, which was pretty much a daily routine. He always announced his presence (he couldn't help it) by clicking his ballpoint pen as he walked, or rather stormed, through whatever space he was in. Under our breath, we called him "Clicky."

I steered as clear away as possible, but it was hard considering we had a lot of in-house meetings that always seemed to include Marketing. Clicky was at most of them, always critical of something minute like the footer of a font but never offering suggestions. The section managers yessed him to death but afterward told us not to worry about what he said. For some unknown reason, we were untouchable; most of our mockups got shepherded through with very little outside manipulation and became our magazine ads, banners for trade events, and social media reels.

In his manifesto, submitted on Christmas Eve day— when most of us were bringing on the good cheer early with the usually proscribed plastic cup holding an adult beverage—Clicky bemoaned the supportiveness that he said was being denied him due to his age. This was preposterous because there were people younger and older than him who mentioned no such problems. All of this made sense, though. He was a man always on the edge who looked for opportunities to prove how he'd been wronged, and this latest document attesting to his displeasure came at a time when he was under an intense audit by the AICPA, dreaded by all professional accountants. If he so much as sneezed wrong, it could be escalated to the SEC's Oversight Board. So yeah, he was on edge.

I thought nothing of the audit since our department was not a high-spending one. We stuck to our budget when we needed freelance artists or attended industry events, most of which we did online. In fact, we had to fight our sup tooth and nail to get an ad run. She was miserly and proud of it, and that kept Robert Wheatfield out of our hair.

After Christmas break, I had forgotten all about his manifesto, but one day, Danny Ackerman, our company nurse, cornered Bernie and me in the tiny kitchen.

"He's gone but left a stink." Danny stood with his arms crossed, waiting for us to ask him what he was talking about.

"I'll bite," I said. "What happened to who?"

"Robert failed the audit and he's out of here. However, not before mentioning every one of us in his stupid manifesto."

"He mentioned the art department?" Bernadette asked warily.

"See for yourself. Frank in Ops sent it to me on the QT and told me to delete it immediately, but naturally, I couldn't figure out how to do that." Danny gave us a sardonic look. "I have a copy if you want to see it."

"Nah," I answered for the both of us.

Bernie wasn't so sure. "Just read the part about us," she said. "Unless it's really hateful. I trust your judgment."

"Okay: 'The Art Department is run by a blothering'—his typo, mind you—'idiot who has no regard for our bottom line. The supposed trade shows were nothing but a mockery of professionalism and the two morons who work for her can't design a business card, let alone a corporate branding.'"

"Obviously, he thinks *very highly* of us." I nodded to Bernie. "Go on."

Danny put on a high-pitched, officious voice and continued. "'Berndice'—again, his error, not mine—'and Phyllis can never seem to agree and have caused additional meetings at the company's ongoing expense, even asking for lunch to be served during one of them.'"

"Liar!" I shot out.

"Phyl, who cares? He's gone." Bernie squeezed my shoulder.

"I don't need to hear any more of this crap. My break is O V E R, over. Bye, kiddies."

"That was it for Art," Danny called after me. "He did rip *me* a new one, though. Maybe you want to hear it, Phyllis?"

"You can tell it to me," Bernie answered, watching me go back to our office.

The stress and tumult that Robert Wheatfield caused by his silently judgmental walk-throughs had stopped—thank goodness—and in its place was a gregarious older woman who seemed extremely grateful to have been hired. She was a sweetheart. Without divulging much about her predecessor, I promised her that our department was very "bottom-line oriented" and that we were all very happy to have her on board.

Four months later, word came through our daily paper that Clicky had found himself in legal trouble. He'd been hired by a firm in another state and was caught stealing supplies, up to and including a desktop color printer. He'd sure gone up in the world from the humble ballpoint pen.

Second-Hand Squeeze Box

Forty-two years ago, the clerk of the Circuit Court of Kings County sent me the letter that would change my life forever. I was now (it said) officially divorced. As I embarked on my new journey, leaving the ex and his philandering ways behind, I decided to treat myself to something really special.

A clarinet.

I had wanted to noodle along with our Glenn Miller records since taking a sixth-grade class trip to the Brooklyn Museum. There was a small ensemble performing in the atrium, and from the very second I heard the clarinet's mournful tone threading through the hallways of the adjoining Egyptian exhibit, I was hooked. Frankie Joya, my harried classmate and the school's favorite soloist, played it like a dream, and I basked in my own dream of doing a personal duet together. If only I could learn it, maybe he'd notice me. Those days—and that music—imprinted on my soul.

I joined band in seventh grade (I was assigned the tuba, which was completely absurd because of my size), but by that time, the Joya family relocated to New Jersey. I never did get to play the clarinet, but I sure loved all the Benny

Goodmans and Artie Shaws of the world. Plus of course Buddy Rich and Sammy Davis Jr., but drums were not about to happen in the Goldman household.

And now, newly single, I had my full-time job that paid well enough to stay in the apartment without the second income. As long as the City of New York's County of Kings needed an expert recruiter who could understand the inscrutable civil service lists, I'd have a (rented) roof over my head and food in my (landlord's) behemoth fridge. Landlord nosiness notwithstanding—they saw my ex move out and bluntly asked if I could still afford the apartment— I would remain there and breathe the air of a free woman. I started putting away a few shekels toward that clarinet. The plan was to hop on the D train to Music Row in Midtown Manhattan for a suitable starter instrument, but then Jessy, my best friend since junior high, suggested a pawn shop.

I was horrified. Only desperate people went into those places. After all, it was the gritty '80s in NYC. I wasn't gonna do that. But when I saw that Sam Ash's "bargain basement" instruments started at $1,200—and that was low, compared with the other music retailers that were abundant in the city—my clarinet dreams died on the vine.

Life got busy; I eventually met somebody new. That didn't take either. It was time to make a change, so I broke out of Brooklyn and edged westward, settling in nearby Pennsylvania. I had also pivoted in my career and was now a recruiter for a mega university, a soulless if not well-paid way to resent my life and occasionally wish for my own demise. I had not the time nor the energy to twaddle away on the clarinet.

Until Jessy—who'd moved to the next town over— shared her addiction to antiquing and thrifting and asked me to come with her on her next trip, which she did on Tuesdays for their weekly discounts.

"What do you buy?" I asked.

"Anything from Occupied Japan."

I took a beat. "Like…what kinds of things?" I didn't want to seem ignorant but apparently I was. Did she mean wartime stuff?

Dishes, she told me: glassware, housewares. Hand-painted, delicate, a story in every object.

"Maybe you'll find that clarinet you've always dreamed about." Jessy bribed me with a local dinner, her treat, and the latest gossip on her co-worker's affair with her neighbor. I'm not above such discussions.

The former hunting shack I moved into in Stroudsburg had been weatherized for year-round living. Modest, yes, but big enough for me as well as one clarinet. I had been missing a creative outlet. Suddenly, that small flame burned a little brighter and I said okay.

I was tired but excited. Every evening after work was the same. For me, this counted as high adventure.

We walked into her favorite second-hand establishment. Floor to ceiling pre-owned objects from busted-up rattan chairs to massive midcentury dressers, mirrors that had turned black, countless Tony Bennett albums, and a staggering wealth of well-worn objects (some called it junk) to fit every purpose and desire. We found the instrument section, and there was a clarinet, but in fact it was something else I spied that got my attention. How else to say it but that I got ambushed by an accordion.

I couldn't resist. The mother-of-pearl buttons and deeply folded bellows called out to me from behind glass. It should have been the clarinet next to it that spoke the loudest, but I was smitten by this cute squeeze box.

I summoned the store manager, and he came over with a jingling ring of keys that shimmered under the fluorescent lights. When he slid open the glass panel and took out the instrument, he said, "You better sit down."

Why? It's like 11 x 17. I can hold that in one hand.

Jessy quickly brought over a chair, which I started to scoff at, but she pushed me into it. Just in time, too. The manager hefted it over and nearly knocked me down.

"They call this a squeezebox?" Its weight shocked me. "This is a monolith. How does anybody hold this upright, let alone get any music out of it!"

Maybe it was a mistake. Certainly the svelter clarinet wouldn't dent my thighs like this.

"Do you know how to play?" he asked. But I think he already knew the answer.

"No, but I have YouTube."

The little tag dangling from one of the straps said it was $95. "I'll give you $85."

I'd never haggled in my life. I was trying to get a rise out of Jessy, who nearly choked, and honestly, I was half kidding. To my surprise, the guy grunted and said to bring it up front.

Drag it up front was more like it.

Jessy had found a few teacups and an ashtray to add to her glassware at home. She knew exactly what they were worth and told him what she was going to pay. He could tell she was an informed collector.

"There's just one thing," he told me as I struggled to place my new baby onto the counter to pay.

"What is it?"

"The owner, he wants me to call him if I sell it. Said he wants to be sure it's going to a good home."

I didn't want to give out my name or info. Maybe I should stick with the clarinet. "Do you have to say exactly who's buying it?"

"No, but..."

This was getting slightly weird. I waited, re-considering the other instrument I'd so callously ignored. Visions of the dark-eyed, thirteen-year-old Frankie Joya danced in my head. He was playing a *hora* from the days of the shtetl. Why, I had no idea.

"Well...why not. Just tell him it's going to a dumpy old lady whose life will finally be given meaning by its very existence."

Jessy shook her head.

Dinner was great: tempura at a local Japanese restaurant. The gossip about our coworkers was ridiculous; we laughed like we were superior to them and had never screwed up in our own lives. But I needed to be up early the next day for some new fun at the office.

When I got the accordion home to my tiny abode, I set it down on the dresser. After being wiped down, it glistened appreciatively. I admired every little valve, crease, and screw. "It's just you and me, kid," I said aloud, inexplicably in a Jimmy Cagney voice.

Workdays were so busy that after clocking in something like two hundred mostly unintelligible resumes from healthcare hopefuls, I decided to wait until the weekend to start in with my new little musical friend.

On Saturday, I fired up my laptop and watched a few videos on how to hold the accordion and what the different buttons and keys did. It was a beauty. I had a good ear and was going to try something easy. Maybe "Amazing Grace." By now, I'd certainly forgotten about the instrument's former owner whom I'd mentally dismissed as a "needy little golem." Imagine having something for sale at a thrift store and asking the owner to make sure it goes to a good home.

Then my phone buzzed.

"Hello?"

"Ms. Sharon? This is Ralph from A-Town Antiques in the Lehigh Valley."

"Uh, hi." I took a deep breath, bracing for whatever was coming next. "What's up?"

He cleared his throat. "I'm calling about the accordion you purchased. The owner. He wants it back. He said he'll pay you double for it."

This was clarinet karma right here.

"What? Why?" I just needed a moment to process.

"He said it's a family heirloom and he really meant to take it down. And he's very sorry."

Was I attached to it yet? Or just the idea of it? I let the silence force a further explanation.

"In fifty-five years, this has never happened," he continued. "I'm sorry. But you have every right to say no. I only told him that I'd try, is all."

"Is that clarinet still there?"

"Yeah. It's $75. And with the owner paying you back double, you'll make out. You can get the clarinet with change to spare. Should I put it aside for you?"

I told him I'd be there tomorrow.

At first, I was annoyed. Jessy, however, was outraged and told me to tell the golem and the owner of the store where to stick it.

"That would hurt. It's decidedly bulky."

"Sharon, this is unbelievably unprofessional of them. I think you call him back and tell him you changed your mind. You're gonna keep it."

I didn't need the trouble. The owner had my phone number and I had no idea if he would share it, even though I expressly told him not to. I wasn't too deep in. To Jessy's great disappointment, I told her I lost the feeling and just wanted to be done with it. She said she understood; I should do whatever I thought was best.

"You'll come with me to bring it back?" I asked.

"Of course."

The next day, we set out at around 11:30 since they had Sunday hours and didn't open till noon. I wanted this behind me. I'd have my long-awaited clarinet after all.

The old man recognized me the moment I walked in. Well, that and the fact that I was shlepping a gleaming white accordion.

"You kept your word," he said.

"What else is there in life," I said, no question posed.

He came out from behind the counter, took the squeeze box, and headed for the instrument cabinet.

Just then, a strikingly handsome man walked into the store. "Gary!" he called out to the owner. "Hang on, I'll take that off your hands."

Jessy elbowed me in the ribs. "Guess who's here! I think he wants to meet you."

"Stop," I whispered. "He's bizarre. Those eyes, though."

Gary walked over to the counter and this very fit specimen of a man followed him. He smiled at me.

"You're the one who bought this?"

I nodded. My face and neck started getting warm. I was mortified at my body for its betrayal.

So what if he's a looker? He's a weirdo!

"Gary, so that's your name," I said to the owner, deftly ignoring the way the new guy's shaggy salt-and-pepper hair framed his perfect face.

"Let me get you the clarinet and the rest of your refund," Gary said.

We got settled up and Jessy and I turned to go out the door. She ignored a gilded Japanese plate that caught her eye as we neared the exit. She smiled at me and patted the clarinet case. "Time to skedaddle." She was a true friend.

Just then, a husky voice called after us. "Ladies, can I take you to lunch?"

I turned to see chocolate brown eyes looking at me quizzically. Before I could figure out what I wanted to do, Jessy decided for me. For us.

"You got us all the way out here to Allentown on a Sunday, so yeah, you can take us to lunch." She beamed at him.

At this point, I didn't know if she thought this guy was good for her or for me. I had no horse in this race. A free meal was a free meal. We walked three blocks east to a diner.

This was turning out to be one of the strangest Sundays ever.

We slid into the diner bench, Jessy and I facing off against Mr. Accordion.

"My name's Mike Schrager, by the way. I just really wanted to thank both of you. I happened to be there when you returned the Hohner."

"So did Gary tell you I was returning it today?" I grilled him. "Or were you basically stalking the store, waiting for us to appear?"

Mike gave a little mock frown. I instantly hated him. I hated the way something stirred inside me. I also wasn't comfortable having this feeling with Jessy next to me and not knowing where she weighed in. She seemed at least amused; I couldn't tell if she *like*-liked him or what. But I'd defer to her. I was happy enough without a man to complicate my life.

"Well, for that—again—I'm sorry. Can you ever forgive me?"

"I'm frankly not sure yet." I smiled tightly.

Jessy pushed her leg into mine. *Be nice,* it said.

After some highly charged banter, we finished lunch and Mike peeled off. "See you around sometime."

I knew how cute Jessy and I were, and the fact that he didn't press us for our numbers was actually surprising…and refreshing. I'd lost an accordion but gained a clarinet and a free meal.

Two weeks later, I went back to Gary's store. I wasn't looking for anything in particular, but a vintage brass music stand caught my eye. I ambled over to it. The tag read $55 with the name "M. Schrager" scrawled underneath. Maybe he'd want this back, too. At this point, I wasn't convinced that was necessarily a negative.

I found Gary in the baseball card section. I took a deep breath and let it out in a hiss. "Will you take $50 for that music stand?"

Poems

Dragged Triplets

Crinoline
What it takes
Come right here
Beat the band
Beat some eggs
Justify
Melody
Speed it up

Jazzy times
Come to pass
Cardinal
Robin's nest
Stomp the foot
Tap your toes
Run in place
Rhythm-rich

Layer cake
Port-au-Prince
Fabulous
Dragonfly
Honey pie
Eat dessert
There ya go
Y'all come back

Bookishness
Author name
Plot - subplot

Writing soul
Musical
Interview
Characters
Dialogue

Off the beat
Drag 'em out
Cut away
Slice of pie
Play it loud
Soloist
Get the mood
Swing it hard

Jazzy times
Grab a sax
Trumpet plays
Bass trombone
Clarinet
Keyboards, man
4/4 time
Smoky club

The Mirror

How have I aged?
With aggravation and adaptation
An eye on my career and professional veneer
With stumbles and fumbles and all kinds of errors.
Times I faced head-on, frankly terror-fied.
And I've had pride...
Sometimes too much.

How have I conducted myself?
Sometimes with grace.
Other times, I lost face.
Totally avoidable, the not being nice.
I'd look in the mirror and take a look twice.
Snap to and remember:
Kindness goes a long way.

How many trips around the Earth?
I'm getting into the higher numbers now.
But blue jean jeggings and
Big T-shirts with black leggings,
a chipper optimism
and love to keep me warm.
That's kept out the storm.

Why is time accelerating?
It's a mobius strip.
The weeks are twisted, compressed
Leaving me stressed
Trying to squeeze in every last drop.
That was before.
Tomorrow? Do more.

What's our legacy?
Kindness, compassion, creativity.
Making a path
Deciding fast
I'm just trying out ways to leave my mark.
It could be my Polaroid shots
or story dialogue—I have lots.

How will I age?
I can look to my parents, or
self-examine my actions,
disregard the distractions.
Stay focused on good health.
Movement, altruism, fresh air
Clear mind and affection to share.

I'm watching the cells die
In real time.

Deal 'Em

Clear the decks, clear the table
Our monthly card game is about to begin.
I crack my knuckles and smile at my opponents.
Kindred poker spirits.
I've recently met them and have been invited into their game.
I accept with grace and humility
Thankful for being included…
And here I was saying I had no friends.

Amid half-sandwiches
Sinfully rich mac and cheese
And salads for acid and balance—
Also keeping in mind the host's incredible assortment of teas
straight from the UK.
Not in bags, but mindfully curated and pressed lightly into a tea ball.
I must let it steep, I'm told;
No early extractions allowed!
We settle in, rearrange our hands, sort by suit
or place in number order.
I always seem to attract low pairs.

Sixty years earlier,
Around a table 300 miles away
Peopled with my Brooklyn ancestors
I recall games that were loud/veering on aggressive,
at least to a six-year-old's mind:
Uncle Mel slapping the table and yelling at my dad for his skillful bluff

Aunt Ruth admonishing her husband Sam for folding too
soon
My mother and grandmother puffing away on their fat
Parliaments.
No matter that I'd taken to hiding all their cigarettes:
I'd be yelled at and told to bring them back N O W.

This group around this table here
We don't smoke
We don't yell
We tell stories of our gardens and our grown kids who have
moved away.

I still need a cheat sheet for poker
to know what beats what
But I know the basics and bluff often,
like my dad.

Today, first hand in, I have two pairs with a queen high.
We'll break for lunch
after each of us has had a chance to deal.
I can shuffle like a pro
Tent the cards and let them fall in together
in perfect collation.
A knee-jerk reaction as a small smile comes to my lips.
I'm recalling an old memory also set around a poker table
When cigarette smoke clouded the air
And when bagels and sable and whitefish
With red onions
Were what they broke for.

24-Hour News Cycle

Hey you.
I see what you did there.
I notice that you left
a trail of breadcrumbs.
Doesn't mean that I have to follow it.

It's bad enough
that there's a wild game of pinball
going on in my head.
And now you feel compelled to infiltrate my peace?

I'm going to be my own activist
in the search for joy.
So, you've been evicted.

Acquiescence

The pleasure center that lives in my brain woke me up abruptly at 1:30 in the morning,
just for the pleasure of traumatizing me.

Bacon, it sang. *Get up and make me some bacon.*
Preposterous, ridiculous, and I will not kowtow to these random attempts to ruin my calorie tracking for the day ahead.
So that's a NO.

You can make it quietly, my brain continued.
No need to wake everybody up.
Just a slice or two. A nice, thick, juicy slice. And maybe a fried egg.
And put that on one of the gourmet buns you just got from Publix.

I sure know how to talk myself into something…
This sounded great.
Could I be quiet about it?
I started thinking of the salty goodness on the pillowy bun
And how an egg would be the perfect complement.

There was no way in hell
To make bacon
And do it smelllessly.
Impossible, impractical, and I refuse to give in to such a whim.

Wellll,
my brain continued on its path of self-torture,
What about the news? The story you've been following.

You know the one. The one you've been talking to your therapist about nonstop.
We could think about that instead.

Bastard! You sure know how to hurt a gal.

If bacon can stop my catastrophizing
Bring on the nitrates.

On the Lonely Side

She wakes, she stretches, she lights a cigarette.
She goes to the bathroom and remembers
She's 45 and her husband
has just died.
Nobody—in the history of time—
Ever felt so utterly abandoned, empty of one's insides,
Bereft, broken.
Nothing to do but wait it out,
hoping to die one day
And leave the pain.

Systematically, she dismantles each of her friendships,
one by one,
Telescoping so deeply into herself that no light gets in.
Embittered, she doubles down and continues to
self-destruct, making enemies of her only living advocates
—her kids—
and thus poisons the well of motherhood.
Things devolve
And the remainder of her years, originally so ripe with
promise,
are spent with self-loathing, a desire to exit as emotionally
painfully as possible.

I wish I knew then
what I know now:
More kindness was called for.
I failed, in that regard, until the end,
When, just in time, I find some resting in a small puddle at
the bottom of a dried-up well
and we make amends.

Legerdemain

He's a light scientist.
The kind that makes things glow from inner energy.
He excites particles
Causing a rise in temperature
An acceleration of electrical conductivity
The skin's gradual warmth
The dilation of pupils
A soft thrumming of the pulse.

He's a light scientist.
A magician
Practicing sorcery
On my self-containedness.

Thoughts on a Wake

Kind words spoken
by a handful.
Others, silent.

Respect needs to be shown
while they're alive,
not in the post-mortem.

Funeral clothes
refrigerated flowers
ribboned wreaths
all say zilch.

But words unfettered by the darkness
that address the positive aspects of a life…
Those should be our statements.

Try for more integrity
when you speak of the dead.
They might be listening.

Debbie Burke

The Keys

With apologies and thanks to Edgar Allan Poe

Hear the clicking of the keys
Plastic keys
Keys for little dollhouses that open as you please.

Where a child learns the wonder
Of what a key can mean.
An entry into made-up worlds
Different family, different scene.

Hear the small toy keys that your parents kindly offer
Of the make-believe, just-for-pretending keys.

Hear the jangling of the keys
Retail keys
Entrusted only to a few by powers that will be.

Open the store in the morning
And then close it when it's time.
Just hope you never lose them
Or you'll find the unemployment line.

Hear the stainless-steel keys that you only need for working
Of the hold-onto-them, job security keys.

Hear the clanging of the keys
Jailers' keys
For the sentenced, the confined ones
Who have lost their freedom's ease.

Keys you shouldn't dream to touch
So close, but yet so far.
The boulder's weight of punishment
Your soul will bear its scar.

Hear the heft and bulk and gravity, the solemn punishment
Of the life-altering, time-stealing keys.

Hear the cacophony of keys
Locksmith's keys
Who brings them from a hardware store
To secure your home's entry.

Dirty, dusty key machines
The screech of keys when cut.
An object grooved, precision-carved
To fit your front door's lock.

Hear the metal shred and tear, the high-pitched cry it makes
Of the one-of-a-kind, safety-in-mind keys.

Hear the yelling out of keys
Jazzmen's keys
Follow as they modulate
Majors, minors, A through G.

Chords that form arpeggios
Play a solo, improvise.
Riffing off the main theme
Melodies that reach the skies.

Hear the keys, so dissonant, whose music must resolve
From the disordered and strangely rhythmed keys.

Hear the swiftly shifting keys
Railmen's keys
As the train pulls in the station
Doors slide open, people squeeze.

Get off, get on, just mind the gap
And use your quickest step.
Train's about to move again
Its schedule is set.

Hear the keys, so many of them, as they jangle on a chain
Of the stressed and pressed, time-sensitive rail keys.

Hear the whisper of the keys
IT keys
The secret code you're given
For your brain's own memory.

Don't forget: put in a safe place
(or you might be written up).
Take it to your grave, perhaps
Or beneath your coffee cup.

Hear the keys, just don't repeat them, all your logins will depend
On the cryptic, nonsense, workplace BS keys.

Hear the meep-meep of the keys
Electric keys
For your vehicle, to lock it
Fobs need fresh new batteries.

Tap it two or three times
To be sure it's really locked.
Hit the locator to find your car
If it's stolen you'll be shocked.

Hear the keys with which you drive away or return you to
your home
Of the electronic, satellite-dependent keys.

Hear the music of the keys
Your lover's keys
As they fumble with their keyring
And hope the lock agrees.

When they walk in through the front door
And then take you in their arms
Love's a hug, a hearth, a home sweet home,
The house key just a charm.

Appreciate the meaning of a space that's safe and warm
In the place you and your beloved put your keys.

Modern Chemistry

How does lime juice cook shrimp?
It's a thing, they say.

How does the sun know to rise every morning,
all over the Earth?
It just does, they say.

Then indulge me one more.
How does time heal grief?
You can trust it, they say.

Call me a cynic, but
After fifty years
That little girl
Who's done a lot of living—
kids, jobs, dogs, books, friends, lovers, and music;
the fullness of experience—
She still can't shake that loss.

So again I ask:
How does time heal grief?
I'm very disappointed to report
They lied.

Dear Centipede

Why, Centipede
Do you impede
My enjoyment of my own damn kitchen?

Your legs freak me out
There's too many to count
And if you really needed to go so fast, why's your body so
fat?
Can you just riddle me that?

I dare not even read
How you evolved and why.
All's I know
Is you make me scream
You haunt my dreams.

I'm busy right now, but sometime later
I'm gonna call my exterminator
And get rid of the likes of you
Because I don't know what else to do.

I'm sorry, Centipede
That you were designed
To creep people out.
If only you weren't so sneaky
Or maybe if you moved slower…
It would give you more clout.

But end you we must
Before you eat that pie crust
Or sip from our sink

(I also heard you stink!)

O Centipede, dear,
Get on out of here.
You're about to be swatted
You've used up the time allotted.

Single-Minded

His impact was insignificant:
A speck on the thumbnail of a giant
And I couldn't be bothered by his presence.
I had work to do.

His existence was negligible...
A cipher who bore no weight on the world
And I had better things to think about.
I had a life to live.

He was all but invisible and soundless;
You can't see what you don't believe exists
And you can't hear what you dismiss as unintelligible.
I stayed focused on my goals.

When, years later, I learned that he passed
A storm came out of nowhere.
The thunder crackled and I cried.
And I thought I heard him say
"Good job.
Now you don't have to work so hard at ignoring me."

I wasn't ignoring him.
I was taking the path that didn't include him
And there was no room for even his name.

Possum Days

Every day, it seemed
The new species of flower revealed themselves.
Let me explain: we moved into a new home.
Several springs turned into summers.
There bloomed unbelievably fragrant gardenias,
Delicately petaled soft pink tea roses
And even wild blackberries!
Along with this surprisingly lush garden
(which we didn't plant)
Were many species of birds.
And yes, one fat waddling possum.
We kept noticing her going under the gardenia bush.
And then one day, there was a baby
In a small circle, cleared of grass.
But—lifeless.
Mama waddled out alone.
Were there others that lived and left?
She has traveled from…I don't know where
And lives maybe in the marsh nearby
Or in a park.
I wonder if she wants more babies
And has to find a new mate.
I kind of wish she would stay under my gardenias.
There are good vibes around this house
And she's welcome to enjoy them with me.

Thoughts Over Tea

Do I look like the rain to you?
Pouring into your small spaces
Rivers of me finding every corner

Go Ahead, Play the Gardener

The mild fruits, banana, pear, and casaba
And the astringent ones, grapefruit and lime
Have their place and their season.

If you must and if you insist,
Sure, try to grow me in your garden.
Remember: lots of hydration
and
Abundant sunshine.

I can't promise I'll flower for you.
I can't guarantee a cutting will take root.
I will try because you say "it's best this way."

And given some more thought,
I might rebel.
For if you force me to grow with you,
My leaves will come out
Jagged and prickly
A weird color of green
And fragrance missing.

I'm not native to your lands.

All I'll Want

Wheel me to the ocean
Bundled
with an extra scarf
and a blanket covering my lap.

A cup of something warm
and a little sweet.
I can watch the waves through the steam coming off the
cup.

Tell me what you dream
The travels…
Planned and unplanned
The loves of your life
who you'll introduce me to.

Ask me my memories
What I loved about growing up
How I navigated the weaker moments
How I made this life mine.

Mary Ellen

How is one supposed to grieve;
How long a shadow does one's passing leave?

I knew you like a tangent, a secondary player
In my husband's life, and now you're a prayer.

What I remember of you is small but strong
It's of you and your laughter as life took you along.

From what little I heard, there were troubled waters
And all families endure this—all sons, all daughters.

On the eve of your burial, I try calling to mind
The last time I saw you but my brain's left that behind.

Rather than an event, I recall just the feeling
A generous-sized love filling floor to ceiling.

What is said about your life may vary in tone
But for me, I'm respectful, knowing God will judge you on
His own.

Fire in the Sky

A morning sky ablaze in orange
squeezes itself through the miniblinds
and pries open my eyelids,
forcing me to leave my warm, comfortable bed.

No need to rally up the troops:
I'm the last one up
and one of them exclaims
as I hurry to the back door in anticipation,
"It's even better than you think."
He's talking about the slight shimmer spilling onto our walls
Not matching the miraculous quality of the light outside.
And he's right.

How often that the inside
has nothing to do with the outside…
The vibrancy of a ruby-skinned apple
Refuses to take into consideration
Its bruised interior.

It's exactly like a person
who pretends to be your best friend
but doesn't make any time for you
and if, as an experiment, you don't call for a day or two,
you'll just never hear from them again.

It's been two election cycles since
your opinions tore apart two who were as close as sisters.

I blame you, of course
(I have always been the more tolerant one).

All the skies we've missed talking about
because, as it turned out,
your inside didn't match your outside.

Microfiction

The neighbors behind me pulled into their driveway,
headlights blindingly announcing themselves through my
bedroom window.

    Must I be awakened?

He walked the canoe carefully down
the boat ramp.
When it was wholly in the water,
he gingerly climbed into it.
He pushed off with one oar
and, once he knew he was floating,
allowed his fingertips to trace circles into the mud-green
water.
Then, plunging in with both oars,
he began his getaway.
Dinner was in three hours…
enough time to get to the end of the reservoir
and turn around to come back home.
Enough time
To think
To decide if his marriage was worth saving.

They wasted my time in the interview,
perseverating on my gap in employment.
"I started a business," I said in my defense.
The recruiter puckered her lips,

Then sighed. It was not done silently.
Why was I subjecting myself to this?
It was as wasteful as
pouring wine down the drain.

"You know," said the horn player, "take a step back and let
the music breathe. It's like playing the Hungarian Dances at
half-speed."

"I don't think you can get an ethical musician to do that," I
replied.

Actually, *you* worked for *me*.
Why in the world would I risk my job?
But I did. I started it all.
One day, our eyes met.
We walked out together
to our respective subway stations.
And your smile lingered
as if already you knew my heart.

The virile smell of coffee in the morning
hits me like a ton of sexy bricks

The dream came and went
Like a prowler leaves shadows
And I didn't get a chance to actively take part in it.

All I wanted was to have a lucid dream
And all it got me was
My own voice telling me
To get up and go to the bathroom.

I pushed a few crumbs off my plate, not prepared for any of this to erupt into conversation. Now that the genie was out of the bottle and he knew I'd fallen in love with somebody halfway around the world, I had to face the music.

"I realize this is my doing. But why did you ignore all the signs and just let us go on like this? Why say something about it now?" I asked, already fearing that my new lover might reject me; that I was much more appealing when I belonged to somebody else.

"In matters of the heart, very often, there's no explanation," he said. "I just feel bad that it took me pressuring you to confess."

I stared at the edges of my toast, unbuttered, unloved, and dry, like our marriage.

He cleared his throat. "I'm sorry you were so hard on yourself, and that you felt like I drove you away, into somebody else's life. But that's not fair to me. So today's breakfast…."

I looked into his tired, gray eyes. He'd been crying. His face was swollen. There wasn't a shred of embarrassment as the tears made trails down his cheeks.

"This"—he gestured to our plates—"is my goodbye to you. I'm very sad you found somebody else, but what is infinitely worse is that you felt you couldn't trust me with this information so each of us could at least have gone forward with dignity."

As he got up to leave, he shook his head. He looked like he was about to say something else, maybe something to remember him by, but he stayed silent. He took the check, walked to the cashier, and paid the bill, then left.

I noticed his socks didn't match. I noticed he stood taller and straighter than I expected him to. I noticed that as he walked out, he didn't look back.

I reached over to his plate for a piece of his toast. I took a bite. He'd gotten rye. Infinitely better than the white bread I ordered. I took out my phone to call my boyfriend, tell him I was finally free.

The recorded message informed me that the number was not in service.

He loved his pungent squares of black liquorice.
He chewed them until they blackened his teeth and gums
and made his breath medicinal.
He also loved peanut chews,
Risking the sticky removal of a worn silver filling
and peanut breath.

My dad didn't smell of alcohol.
He smelled of candy.

We are borrowing time
Like a library book.
One day
We'll have to give it back.

God made you from stardust
From fragments of a million suns
Glints of light
Shards of matter.

The day is done and almost forgotten
I take a bite of something rotten

The sheets are scrambled on the bed,
a swirly statement of our shared somnambulism.
At first light, we decide—wordlessly—not to linger here
But to make breakfast.

I tell Ben, my photographer friend,
there are hundreds of water towers
that squat solidly on city rooftops.
They dot the rural landscape, too;
spindly aliens overlooking towns
promising to deliver water when needed.
How true this is, I can't say.
There have been droughts.

The Meteor Symphony

There was no way to outrun the gun pointed at my face.

The fat guy wielding a .38 aimed it midway between my eyes. He bit onto a slimy cigar while drooling and talking messily through his teeth. I instantly appreciated the importance of paying attention. These could be the last words I'd ever hear. But it was hard to concentrate with the roar of my own terror pulsing through my temples.

"Get on your knees."

The carpet was soggy with urine (my own), but I complied and waited for the worst.

"Now follow my directions carefully, Missy. Very carefully."

Spit.

"You're going to give me what I want, and then you're going to meet your maker."

He took the wet cigar out of his mouth, dropped it near his right foot—landing right in front of me—and ever so gently twisted his toe into it.

I recited the only prayer I knew, which happened to be the Hebrew *hagunah*, asking God to bless the wine. I didn't know the one where you asked for a painless death.

Baruch ata Adenoi, Eloheinu Melech Ha'Olam, borei p'ri hagafen.

And then he collapsed to the floor, knocked out cold from the sudden body-slamming action of two of New York City's finest.

Why I was there in the first place had everything to do with Gustav Holst.

As a cellist in a small symphony orchestra in the depths of Alabama, I made the trip up to New York to purchase a supposedly authentic artifact that came from none other than Gustav Holst. My classical music hero.

It was my first time visiting the Hotel Jerome Ascher on Eighth Avenue in Manhattan. Per our emails, I was to meet this creep in the third-floor lounge right outside the Tulip Ballroom. The lounge looked down on the main lobby two floors below.

According to the Craigslist post, he was selling the first movement of an unfinished symphony by Holst. I was hooked ever since hearing *The Planets* when I was eleven; it was what started me on the cello (by way of a three-quarter size violin). The *Jupiter* movement was the most emotional music I'd ever heard in my life. The lyricism of the main melody that twists and turns sinister and then finally, with a breath from the violas, becomes only the most beautiful few bars ever written in music…that was its pure, shining essence captured in notes. Holst *knew me*, even though generations separated us. The sheet music, if genuine, might hold clues to his process, his inspiration, and might even contain some autobiographical slips that revealed more about who he was.

The Craigslist ad read:

MUST LOVE GUSTAV HOLST. I'm selling the sheet music for the allegro movement of a symphony signed by Holst. It's called The Meteor Symphony. Unknown even by the scholars. Full orchestra score, 6 pages. Small print and hard to read. Unfortunately, I have Stage 4 lung cancer and so now this needs a good home. Bring USD $1,200 in cash and we'll meet in midtown

Manhattan. Private buyers only. No corporations or capitalists.

I fit the profile and wrote back. I could squeak by with $1,200. I'd just gotten a tidy little bonus at the Southeast Alabama Symphony. My finger was itching to respond before anybody else could grab this piece of history. I made up a new email address for privacy's sake and told him I'd be there at an agreed-upon date and time. Then, I put in for a week off. The timing was just right—it was between seasons and we wouldn't be reconvening for rehearsal for another two weeks.

As for checking the authenticity, the seller agreed to send a photo of a few sections of the music that he posted on Craigslist at an appointed hour before taking them down. I had to make sure to grab screenshots to examine them at my own pace.

Graphology was somewhat of a side hobby of mine. From what I knew about Holst's handwriting (deep, skinny-looped descenders, rounded, almost childlike capital Ls), I felt confident that the documented style matched the photos.

I won't lie, though. This was definitely shady. Otherwise, he would have gone to an auction house where I'm sure it would have fetched in the tens or hundreds of thousands. Obviously, there was a reason he was going on the QT here.

If it was authentic, I'd have a unique piece of music history. I tried to weigh the risks. What was the worst that could happen? We would be meeting in a public area in the busiest place in the country, New York City, my old hometown. I was obsessed. The notion of getting ripped off aside, I knew I had to take the chance. Surely this was a once-in-a-lifetime opportunity, I told myself.

The cops galloped up the stairs from the lobby and found me in a ball, rocking myself on the carpet, which was now starting to smell.

The crowd that formed around me was shrieking. I couldn't keep a straight thought and began wailing. I think I was in shock.

A female cop knelt down by me and beamed a Cheshire Cat smile. My heart was beating out of my chest and my brain was encased in molasses. She managed to keep me calm. I reached up to her for a hug. I do not enjoy physical contact with strangers, so I must have needed the connection. Unspeakable fear. Emotional trauma. And the relief of still being alive.

But where was the Holst??

"Miss, is this yours?"

I must have shoved the manuscript into my purple paisley duffel bag that a male cop was now holding out to me. He had teeth like perfect Chiclets, distracting me from my wild-eyed anxiety.

"Yes. Thank you." I took it and sat on it to try to hide it.

I'd paid the seller for half of it online via a very convoluted purchase of a gift card that had to be applied to a phony GoFundMe. Then I finished today's transaction by handing off the balance in cash right before things turned horrific.

"We may want to take a closer look at that," said the officer, nodding a chin at the bag underneath me. "But let's get you checked out by EMS." Then he took my information and a statement.

The EMS people pressed through the crowd, and a fresh-faced woman in a white blouse showing her company emblem carefully helped me up. "Do you want to go to the ER?"

No, I didn't. But I knew enough about health insurance from my left knee replacement to document every possible injury in case there were complications later on.

Knowing what my wait time might be here in the center of Manhattan but also understanding that my judgment was going to be impaired by the situation, I answered, "OK. Where's the nearest one?"

"Two blocks away." She held up a hand for me to stop talking and fitted a Velcro cuff around my wrist. Surprisingly, my blood pressure was normal. Her colleague, a young man with a soft-looking beard that was tied off in a ponytail, pulled up a fancy overstuffed chair, one of several around the perimeter of the hotel lounge. He helped ease me down onto the cushion.

Vitals good, I told them I'd walk or take a cab to the ER.

"We can take you."

My insurance from the symphony was top-notch, so the transport would be covered after paying a small deductible; the ER visit would be what it would be. I had no complaints in life other than, of course, having recently stared down the barrel of a handgun and knowing my bladder had lost control, for which thankfully somebody had given me a sweater to tie around my waist.

"Let me get to the bathroom and I'll be right back," I said.

I remembered about my duffel bag and put the strap crosswise on my body, feeling inside frantically for the Holst as I had immediately forgotten I checked for it not a minute ago. It was still in there, loosely rolled and rubber-banded. I ducked into the nearest restroom and came out in record time, four minutes. I wanted to be done with the police and out of the Jerome Ascher.

"Ma'am, would it be okay to take some pictures of your music there?" the police officer with the perfect pearly whites asked.

I handed over the manuscript and he took pictures quickly, then returned the rolled-up pages with his business card.

"Feel free to contact me if you think of anything else."

I nodded, but as far as I was concerned, I had nothing left to say and wanted to move on with my life.

By now, the other officer had yellow-taped the area to keep back the gawkers. The Craigslist animal, who just came to, was aggressively cuffed and then roughly escorted outside into a waiting squad car. I never saw anything like it in all my years as a New Yorker, even though the Big Apple always held the threat of criminal elements.

When I had turned thirty, I made the move to southern Alabama. I wanted out of the Northeast's slushy, bitter winters and out of the two-fare zone of my daily commute into the city. Why Alabama? The Opelika Symphony Orchestra was the only professional outfit to offer me a job. And in less than a week, I would head back to my sweet southern home where there were no cigar-sucking bad guys waiting for their marks in hotels.

Maybe I could convince the conductor to have us play the new Holst, even just to run it as a lark. That is…if it was authentic.

After a modest—for New York—three-hour wait, the ER doc gave me a clean bill of health, so I was free to wander the streets of New York or return to my own hotel across town from the hospital and far from the hotel of horror. I decided I'd check in and throw myself in bed.

I didn't need to be back in Opelika for another six days. A lot could be accomplished in that stretch of time, and I had most of it planned out. What I didn't plan for was almost being killed, but now that was water under the George Washington Bridge.

Part of my research before coming north was finding experts in musical notation and antique manuscripts. The closest one was in New Haven, Connecticut, and the best way to get there was Amtrak, which would be tomorrow's day trip. Dr. William Judson, stationed for the past three years at Yale on a grant from the National Endowment for the Arts, said he would do his best to help. His office was just off campus, and he was staying in a rented historic home nearby, paid for by the grant.

Judson was a scholar, an author, and an expert in nineteenth- and twentieth-century music. He told me he also used to play bass. Thanks to the knuckleheaded felon who posted (then quickly removed) a few fuzzy photos of the music, I promptly emailed the images over to my new Yale connection, who enthused that he was definitely on board to help me decipher the marginalia and other scribbles that maybe-Holst had made. His first impression was that these weren't instructions for the musicians—not a guidebook for dynamics or pace—but something else. I was of course excited about what tomorrow's visit would bring.

It was still a stunning day in the city, the kind where the sun glints off the chrome of tall buildings, but I was spent. Nothing wrong with decompressing given the recent circumstances, so after a hot but weak hotel shower, I put on sweats and ventured outside. New York City has more delis than people, it seemed, so I treated myself to takeout: a dozen glistening pieces of sushi and a mammoth black and white for dessert, then I walked two blocks back to the hotel. Four in the afternoon was not too early to start hunkering, not after the freaky day I'd had.

Tomorrow, I would have a fresh outlook on life, smell better, and be ready to get some questions answered about the musty music manuscript safely ensconced in my duffel bag.

Amtrak obliged with no hitches in my travels, and I arrived in New Haven at 11:30 a.m. as expected. Finding a

Victorian mansion in the middle of the Yale campus was not hard. Dr. William Judson was right; it was a short walk from the train.

There was already a man out on the porch. The good doctor, I assumed.

"Miss Marley," he said, extending his hand. I shook it. He had a very firm grip. Strong fingers from playing bass, I assumed.

His office smelled manly—the requisite leather couch with faceted rivets, wood paneling, the sweet smell of old books, but also something else. On a side table were vase upon vase of fresh flowers, giving off a tangled mass of fragrance. A gardener?

He noticed my glance and addressed the floral notes in the air. "I have a, um, friend who brings me whatever's in bloom."

I caught that. Good for him.

"She prunes and I benefit."

I smiled, but at the same time, felt nervous about what he was about to say regarding the Holst.

I sat across from him in a squeaky polished leather chair, slipping from side to side in its immensity. I leaned forward and held out the music while relating the recent events.

"How horrifying!" he said. "So then it's even more of a miracle that you are able to bring this to me today. Thank you for that."

He took out a hefty magnifying glass that made the eyes behind his own thick glasses look inhumanly big. I held my breath.

"These symbols you mention. I saw them in the scans you sent over. They're very familiar."

"Oh?" I said, hoping this was good news.

"But not for the reasons you're thinking." He removed the magnifier from his face and sighed. "I can't be sure, but it's very curious. My ex-sister-in-law collects vintage dream catchers, particularly of the indigenous Native American people of Canada. Some of these are…well, here. Look."

He'd printed out the images I sent over earlier and was now holding up the second page. "Look here." He pointed to the left margin and then made a *tsk* sound, like he wasn't happy about something.

I looked at him and waited.

"These are characters of the north's Ojibwe people, and they convey nothing that makes sense to me. Curiously, they are mixed with proofer's marks. Basically," he cleared his throat, "nonsense."

My chest deflated like a balloon. "Well, let me ask you something," I said, entertaining a glimmer of a possibility that this might still be legit. "Was Holst into spirituality or religion? Might he have gone against his Christian background and been considering other faiths?"

"Yes."

I sat up straighter.

"But don't get your hopes up. He was very curious about Eastern religions. There is no literature whatsoever to support that he even thought about indigenous cultures and beliefs, least of all in North America."

"How sure are you that it's a fake?" My voice caught in my throat. I hated even asking this.

"I'm 80 percent certain it's not legit. But I really need to spend some time with it. Shall we make a better set of copies here and I can let you know next week?"

That was certainly a reasonable request. He obviously felt bad about letting me down and just wanted to be sure before he gave a final ruling.

"Absolutely. With everything that I've been going through in the past twenty-four hours, anything's possible. Take your time."

He looked relieved. "That will do just fine. And please let me treat you to some New Haven pizza. We're actually known for it. I believe you have earned yourself lunch."

That was invalidation number one. Number two came at 4 a.m. the following day, the only time that Dr. Karol Elgaard, a Holst expert, could hop on a Zoom. Through his thick Hungarian accent, he sounded very excited to take this journey with me.

"So, *vhy'd* you choose me?" Dr. Elgaard's eyes twinkled.

"Well…your work at Sotheby's…"

"Yes, a very long and elegant career. The stories!"

"And you've retired?"

"Yup," he said affably.

I smiled at his attempt at informality.

"But not in my heart," he continued. "I'm still following news items of supposedly 'newly discovered'"—here he put up air quotes—"sheet music as well as doing some consulting work for my colleagues who are still in the biz. As you would say in America."

This time, it was my eyes twinkling. "Yes."

"*Cho* me—I mean, *show* me—what you have. I'm very interested."

I had already sent the screenshots to him the week before. Now, I held up each page, one at a time, letting the light from the laptop filter through.

"Okayyy." He drew it out, thinking about what he'd just seen. "I'd like for you to please hold up the third page again, the one with the word 'lento' on the top. I know you play cello and I don't have to overexplain anything. But yes, the lento passage, please."

I complied. Then I noticed something. A twitch in the corner of his mouth supplanted the smile.

He sat back and waved it away. Not impolitely, but sadly. "I'm afraid to tell you that you have a fake."

My eyes widened and I dropped the page onto my lap. "What? Where—how can you tell?"

"AI can do masterful things today. Take for example, forging a signature, an entire body of handwriting, and there are other clues."

Tears sprang to my eyes. Twelve hundred dollars later and I had a fake? Judson hadn't been sure, but this sounded damning.

"The biggest tell, I am afraid, is the watermark. Look about five inches below the 'lento' again. Put it closer to your screen and look through the paper. I'll wait."

Oh no. I saw it.

CONFIDENTIAL

How didn't I notice this before? I argued with myself. *When was I supposed to see this, like, right before he pulled a gun on me?* As if there were time for me to examine this. No wonder that piece of human garbage was in a terrible hurry.

And now he was in jail, or soon to be. So there was that.

"This is most definitely on modern paper, professionally aged. Woven, if you will, to simulate something a century old. I'm sorry." He closed his lips together in a grim smile.

I was furious. Not with him, not even with the forger. With myself. It would make a good story one day, but today, I was a buffoon, an idiot of the first order.

"Can I tell you something that will make you feel better?" he asked.

"Sure. But if there's a $1,200 listening prize, I'm all the merrier."

He guffawed. "No, but in 1979, my early days at Sotheby's, there was an absolutely massive canvas supposedly of one of Keith Haring's proteges. I was younger, yes, and stupider, yes, but also greedier. I also 'calculated'"—air quotes again—"the likelihood of such a big bold work of art supposedly being the work of a man no older than sixteen. I had doubts from the start but wanted it to be real so much that I decided to go ahead and take it on. I had, how you say it, balls."

That would be how I'd say it, yes.

"I presented the work to my superiors, and they laughed at me and said there was no way a teenager did this. My career was just about over," he said. "And then I realized I had better make this right. I took a long, hard look at it and something was off."

"What was the tell?"

"The red."

"You got me. The red?"

"Yup," he said. "I wasn't accustomed to seeing that particular shade of red. So we ordered a lab analysis, such as was available back then. It indicated that the pigment used in the spray paint was only available in Hungary, of all places, and the supposed artist, this kid Phil Androvitz, said he had only bought his cans from his local hardware store, which was in the East Greenwich Village."

"The East Village," I corrected him, but kindly.

"Yes, of course. So this was a small store with very few color choices, and when I called the owner, he said the kid bought all his spray paint there. They got their supply from Sapolin, sourced and mixed in Brooklyn, no ingredients from overseas, period…and certainly nothing even close to that shade of red."

"So you knew it wasn't Phil's?"

"The real artist was an established name from Hungary. Haring had been on a trip there and gifted the canvas to Phil, who then claimed he created it. We tracked down the artist and gave him his own fabulous exhibit."

"You're a fine art detective!"

"I am. But only because I'm an old bachelor and have never had time for a woman, or a man, for that matter. So I have all the time in the world."

The last nail in the coffin came from another in-person visit the next day, this time with a well-known Carnegie Hall fixture. Dr. Cornelia Stanton was not a musician but a "keeper of the music," as she called herself modestly. A master archivist and curator, one of the top in her field. Another source whom it was my good fortune to locate.

We met in one of the city's ubiquitous self-serve delis with an upstairs that looked down on Fifth Avenue.

It was challenging to stay positive after the bad verdicts I'd received from the other two experts, but I didn't want that to color my meeting with Dr. Stanton.

She exuded enthusiasm and looked at my duffel bag almost hungrily. I warmed to her immediately.

"So nice to meet you," I said.

"Same. Thank you for including me in your research. This sounds so exciting!"

We agreed to get our food and find a table upstairs near the huge windows where the sun poured in. I didn't have much hope at this point, but she might have some interesting insights. I decided not to tell her what the others had said and let her come to her own conclusions.

"So, can I see it? I promise not to get mayo on it," she beamed, pushing her tuna on pita aside. We had mashed two empty tables together, a rarity for a New York City lunch, but it was 3 p.m. Not many people had remained in the deli and we were able to spread out.

By now, of course, I wasn't as guarded about the manuscript, so a little mayo wouldn't ruin my day.

I handed over all six pages. She nodded and hummed, sometimes exclaiming a slight "Oh!" and other times closing her eyes and groaning. I couldn't read her but was extremely curious about what else could be wrong with this document.

Stanton took out a loupe and then cocked her head. "I'm sorry."

"I was afraid of that. You're not the only one with bad news for me. So what do you see that's wrong with it?"

"The key changes. They're happening way too many times. D flat minor, G sharp, E, and back to D flat in only five measures. Not only is it terribly uncharacteristic of Holst, but there's something else. Did you know he was in love with an oboist?"

"I vaguely remember reading something about her. I guess it wasn't too unusual for romance to be swirling around in a musical setting. I mean, we go through it in Opelika." Two years ago, there was an embarrassing situation involving a trumpet player and the pianist, both married. "So what about the oboist?" I asked.

"Kilane Elizabeth Morer. She was a quirky woman. All of four-feet-ten. Doll-like in appearance but fierce. More than that. Abusive, it was said, to her lovers."

"Oh boy." By now I was laughing. I was actually relieved that this manuscript was a non-starter; it took all the ambiguity out of the situation. I had already tried on the disappointment and tied a knot in it. But I was certainly up for a good story.

"Do tell."

"Well," she said, grasping her pita and carefully holding in the tomatoes that threatened to spill out. "As you can see, there's barely anything of interest for the oboe to do. And dated as this is, it would have been just about dead center of when he started seeing Miss Morer."

"I see. There's a soaring solo, but it's for the bassoon," I said. "It would have been perfect for the oboe's higher register."

"See? You could do my job."

"I highly doubt it," I said. "But we make a good team, don't you think?"

Two days after I got home and told my tale of woe to my coworkers, our conductor got wind of it and asked me to put it into my music software, filling in the melodies that, he said, were essentially missing.

"Take care of the cellos," he instructed me. "And consider yourself one of the soloists. Then jot down your ideas on the other instrumentation. I'll finish whatever else needs to be done," he added. "I'll pay you $200 for it. We'll play it at our Community Hullaballoo at the end of the year."

I had thoughts churning around the old brain already. The fake Holst had barely used the timpanis and just "phoned in" the basses. I knew what to do and was raring to go.

When the score was complete, we started rehearsals on *The Meteor Symphony*. It sounded phenomenal, just as I'd heard it in my head. The conductor gave me a few free passes for the Hullaballoo that I offered to the two police officers and the EMTs who helped me back in New York City, but they couldn't get the time off to travel to little Opelika. However, I did learn something interesting.

I had never asked why the cops were there in the first place. Everything happened so fast and I was in a panic, considering my own imminent demise. The cretin with the cigar was on a watchlist for fraud, having abused Craigslist for nearly a year as he tried to pass off fake, high-priced antiques to gallery dealers along the Upper West Side. Which only meant that they saw my messages to him as well. Although that didn't sit well with me, I did nothing wrong other than show poor judgment.

The story made the news, but only as an afterthought. Somehow, the authorities had kept me out of it. In fact, Holst wasn't even mentioned by name.

Endnote

Make a plan. Make a roadmap…make a cake, make dinner. Make a will, but only put the really cherished people in it. Or a cherished cause.

Remember your first inner circle. The family you grew up with in the very early days. The neighbors you had, the classmates, even your teachers. Remember the walks around your neighborhood. Maybe you'll move once, twice, or numerous times. Each place has its special flavor and forms a mental picture for you in later years. Some of these places are best forgotten, but most have something important to teach you. Try to be open to the messages they have given you.

I put myself first for so many years. Then I had a family and my kids were first, and then my mother had a series of medical issues and I took care of things with her insurance and her finances. I found that kids grow up and develop their own paths and if you've done any sort of job of yours correctly (as a parent), they'll find their different life paths and meander in their own various directions. You can thank

God that they want to do this. It means they are blessed to have learned from you, and you are doubly blessed to witness this and know they are taking charge of their own lives.

Then…maybe you'll find a new hobby or meet or make new friends. You'll move somewhere smaller and have to find the best coffee shop, the best hole-in-the-wall restaurants; you'll figure out where to find the best live music or take pottery or religion classes. You'll remember that your purpose in being here is to be kind to at least two people: yourself and one other. If you are really accomplished, you will expand that to other people and replicate success wherever you turn or as you have the energy. Pass along the warmth and smiles and you'll be rewarded by seeing happiness reflecting off them.

As the years slip by, you'll worry about misusing your time. That in itself is a time-burner. Pay it no mind. Keep making new plans and delving into things that give you the thrill of being alive. These things will change. Chase them and allow for missteps. Embrace the mistakes because they stretch your character.

For me, it was the following: writing my first book, getting free from a majorly bad relationship, getting my own apartment. Meeting my real match and mate for life and going forward and finding our ways around brand-new cities and towns. It was learning the sax for the first time and playing my first concert; it was a remarkable solo I performed that surprised me and kept me smiling for days.

When the lockdown happened, it was the start of an era of a new kind of PTSD. Thinking about that nearly two-year span makes me remember how we walked around with hollow eyes and hurting hearts. It reminds me of the day we found out John Lennon was killed...of 9-11...and other cultural or political time-markers that ambushed us and impacted us in unpredictable ways.

Eventually, we do snap back. We might have lost a few along the way. Casualties in both the physical sense and the ideological sense. But as long as you're alive and kicking, you'll wake up the next morning and, without resorting to the cliché of "the new normal," get up with a smile, stand tall, make some strong coffee, and face the day with purpose.

Look for opportunities to give love, to show love, to help out, to make somebody smile, to be generous. One day, you'll be too tired for this. When it's winding down, get your stuff in order and thank the people who helped you along in your journey. Let them remember you as a bright flame that said you did life on your own terms.

About the Author

Debbie Burke is the author of twelve books (fiction and nonfiction), mostly about jazz and art. She is also a professional photographer, focusing on architecture, industrial design, and the liminal, as well as a professional editor and author coach at Queen Esther Publishing LLC. Her jazz and photography blog at **debbieburkecreative.com** has garnered international acclaim. Originally from Brooklyn, NY, she now resides in the Tidewater region of Virginia.

Also by Debbie Burke

FICTION

Death by Saxophone
GLISSANDO: A Story of Love, Lust and Jazz
Icarus Flies Home

NONFICTION

Klezmer for the Joyful Soul
Knowing Irv: The Life and Art of Irving Schiffer
Music in the Scriptures
Tasty Jazz Jams for Our Times™ Vols. 1, 2, 3
The Author's Little Red Guide to Editing
The Poconos in B Flat

Amazon: https://bit.ly/DebbieBurkeAuthor
Blog: debbieburkecreative.com
REDBUBBLE: bit.ly/debbieburkephotography
Etsy: queenesther837.etsy.com
Queen Esther Publishing:
queenestherpublishing.com

www.ingramcontent.com/pod-product-compliance
Lightning Source LLC
Chambersburg PA
CBHW070911030726
47504CB00005B/1550